Have you read the prequel short story, *The Night in Lover's Bay*? See how Marcella met the crew of *Eik* and started on her adventure. It's available for free on all retailers.

Also by Liz Alden:

<u>The Love and Wanderlust Series</u>
The Night in Lover's Bay (free prequel short story)
The Fling in Panama
The Slow Burn in Polynesia
The Second Chance in the Mediterranean
The Rival in South Africa (standalone novella)
The Player in New Zealand
The Best Friend in Indonesia (free standalone short story)

<u>Aged Like Fine Wine Series</u>
Rosé with My Fake Fiancé
Riesling with My Roommate
Prosecco with My Professor

Cava with My Colleague

<u>Holiday Retellings Series</u>
Nutcracker with Benefits
Frosty Proximity

<u>Wanderlust Resort Series</u>
Beach Boss (free standalone short story)
Beach Resolution
Put it in Beach Mode

<u>Standalones</u>
The Boudoir Arrangement

THE PLAYER IN NEW ZEALAND

A LOVE AND WANDERLUST NOVEL

LIZ ALDEN

THE PLAYER IN NEW ZEALAND

To anyone who has an ex that deserves a headbutting.
I'm not saying you should headbutt them, but maybe they deserve it.

CONTENT WARNING

This book contains on-page alcoholism and a stalker.

ONE

I'd been around enough bars in the wee hours of the morning to know who was going to be trouble. The group in the back corner, the guys who had been loud, rowdy, and chugging beers all night: they were where I put my money.

Granted, this was a touristy area of Wellington, New Zealand, and a nice bar, the nicest I'd ever worked at. I pulled glasses from the dishwasher and dried them off while the warm wooden wall behind me glowed. The long planks of decorative wood, varnished and gleaming, reflected the tea lights interspersed along the wall. The lights, though electric, were the kind that flickered and impersonated real flames. Paired with the Edison bulbs suspended from the high ceiling and the dark leather of the benches and chairs, the atmosphere here was cozy and inviting.

About half a dozen groups were left and, it being Tuesday evening—I checked my watch. Nope, Wednesday morning—the people here weren't the ones with a lot of responsibilities. Most of the locals had gone home: married people with better things to do than stay out too late, parents with kids who had a babysitter to relieve, or anyone with a respectable job who had to be up in the morning.

Aside from the tourists, mostly obvious from their accents, there was a couple in the darkest back corner, two men. Maybe they were up to something under the table, but that wasn't my place to judge. As long as I was spared an eyeful of private parts, they could go nuts.

Ha. Nuts.

There was a cluster of guys a bit younger than I was—in their early twenties—off to one side of the bar. Ties loosened, sleeves rolled up, they were cocky and confident. My eyes met those of one of the guys as I looked over at their tabletop. They were about due for another round.

He came to the same decision and sauntered over.

"Another round, please," he said, leaning over the bar and giving me a grin. I confirmed the group's beer of choice and pulled from the taps.

"So you're American?" he said, watching me.

I smiled at the beer. "I am."

"How are you liking Welly so far?"

"It's good. I've only been here a couple weeks." I straightened the third beer and placed it in front of him.

A shout came up that pulled my attention to the group that had worried me. One of the guys gestured, eyes wide, palms spread. ". . . and they couldn't catch that hooker. It was complete domination."

I had *thought* that was a sports conversation, not prostitutes and BDSM. But whatever it was, the guys leaned in and their tone dropped and I couldn't hear their responses.

I dragged my gaze back in time to avoid spilling the next beer, and caught the tail end of what this guy was saying to me.

". . . can show you around?"

I started the next beer. "Thanks, but I've got a pretty weird schedule. Work most nights, you know." I smiled ruefully. He was cute, clean-cut, the kind of guy my sister would like. I didn't think I really had a type of my own, but with my tattoos, I seemed to attract this type of guy.

Case in point, his gaze traveled down my face. "I like your nose piercing." He tapped the right side of his nose, where I had a small stud on mine.

"Thanks," I said as brusquely as I thought I could get away with without being rude. I gave him the price for the beers and he handed me his card. When I finished with it, he shoved it into his pocket and picked up all four beers, two in each hand between fingers stretched wide.

"Cheers." He nodded and winked at me, and I sighed in my head. If I were just another patron, I might tell him to fuck off. But on the job, I had to bite my tongue.

That group in the back was still laughing and joking. They were a smattering of guys in polo shirts and shorts, most of them broad-shouldered and tall, crowded around a booth. The ages ranged from guys my age, still looking smooth and polished in their twenties, to a few older men with beer guts and thinning hair. Their skin came in a variety of shades, a few of them white with rosy cheeks and sunburns, a few of them with tanned skin, dark hair and eyes. Most of them had tribal tattoos peeking out on arms and thighs.

My boss was Māori, and I'd guess some of these guys were too.

And they were huge. All of them. If I were back in Boston, I'd say these guys were linebackers. But here in New Zealand, American football was scoffed at.

Helmets! Pads! Weak as!

Kiwis had a charming habit of dropping half of the comparison: *This beer is cold as. That girl is hot as.* Cold as what? Hot as what? The world would never know.

While I had picked up on that linguistic trick, I didn't know what sport was popular around here—between jet lag and job interviews, I'd barely even hung out with other tourists at the hostel.

Then the chanting started. "Oi, oi, oi, oi, oi . . ." Fists pounded the table as they got louder and louder. I glanced over at the bouncer, Ron, seated on a stool at the door, too busy typing into his phone. He glanced up and caught my eye. I flicked my gaze to the rowdy group.

He rolled his eyes. *Harmless*, he mouthed.

I sighed and wiped the top of the bar with a rag. The glass doors overlooking the back deck opened, and a group of middle-aged women came in. Behind them I saw Nina, my manager and the owner of the bar, wiping down tables and putting the chairs back where they belonged under the lights strung up across the yard. That must be the last of the guests outside, so Nina would finish up out there and then relieve me at the bar so I could check out and go home.

"Have a good night," I called out to the group as they passed the bar.

As the ladies strolled past, the crowd of burly men parted and I locked eyes with one of them. He had to be the biggest in the group and he was coming this way. He passed the young business guys and literally stood a head taller than them. As if his height weren't enough, he was broad across the shoulders and all the way down to his thick thighs. The shirt he wore strained at the waist, and the shorts—as was popular in New Zealand—were a touch too short for my American sensibilities.

He also stumbled and blinked. When he paused for a moment just past the group, one of the guys back in the booth called out to him, "Hey, mate, get the shout!"

I expected him to beeline for the counter, but he swerved instead, walking alongside the bar. I glanced at Ron—preoccupied—and followed this beast of a man.

When I realized what he was going for, my stomach dropped.

He got the pass-through open two inches before I slapped my hand down on it. The resulting crack echoed around the room and conversation dipped.

"Sir, you can't come back here," I said. I could have said it more politely, but it was the end of my shift and I doubted this guy was going to back down easily. There was a time and a place for pasting on a smile and bullshitting people, and this was not it.

Though I did smile. Poorly.

Shock passed over his features first. His eyes were dark brown, almost impossible to differentiate from his pupils. His nose was bent and bumped, crooked from a fight or two in his past.

Then his eyes narrowed. I narrowed mine right back. Even at my height—five foot ten, add another two for my boots—I was tilting my chin way up to look at him. It just meant I had to glare harder.

His hand snaked under the bridge, but he maintained eye contact with me as if daring me to protest again. The wood wiggled as he pressed up. I slammed down again with both hands this time, pretty sure that if he decided to use his two giant paws, I'd be screwed. "Sir"—I gritted my teeth—"you can't come back here."

The whole group of men was behind him now. I didn't know which one of the dumbasses in the back started laughing, but soon they all roared at us. This guy's brown skin flushed with embarrassment, a scowl inverting his mouth.

"She's a twig. You gonna let her tell you what for, mate?" someone goaded him.

"Don't stand between him and his beer, sweetheart."

The pass-through slammed open and I snatched my hands back just in time to keep them from getting smashed.

Oh shit.

I stepped forward, shouting for Ron.

"You!" Mr. Big and Tattooed pointed a finger in my face.

"Bloody Americans," someone muttered.

I took a step toward the man as he tried to crowd into my bar. "Sir—"

He stood toe-to-toe with me. "Don't you know who I am? You want to lose your fucking job?"

"Why you importing them anyway, Tane? Hire a proper fucking Kiwi," someone in the back whined. Beyond the group, I caught a glance of Ron trying to push through to me.

Before I could make a retort, the Hulk leaned down to my level. "I'm your fucking boss. Get the hell out of my bar."

Double shit.

TWO

"Tane Taumata!" Nina's sharp voice cut through the noise. "What the hell are you doing? You, get back! Russell, call yourself a fucking Uber and get home to your wife. Ari, I'm going to tell your mother you've overstayed your welcome. All of you, go home!"

I heard a few whines and maybe even a whimper as the men tried to escape. I caught sight of a brown feminine hand poking and prodding, jabbing at soft spots and pinching when necessary.

Finally she got up to me and this Tane guy. Her hand reached up and snatched his ear, twisting and bending him down to her height—not much shorter than I was.

"What the fuck are you doing?" she seethed through her teeth.

He grimaced, twisting in an attempt to escape. "Getting a beer!" He punctuated it with a foreign curse word.

"You are causing trouble, is what you are doing. If our family could see you right now, our dad, how disappointed do you think he'd be, hm? The mighty Tane Taumata, yelling at a woman." She scoffed and pushed his head. He leaned away, but went over too far and stumbled toward me. The drinks had hit him hard—I made a note to myself that the other bartenders had been overserving him—and I took a step forward to try to balance him just as he nose-dived into me.

His shoulder checked me right in my throat and we tumbled down. I gasped for breath and everything stopped. The Hulk was dead weight on me, but because we were at the end of the bar, we didn't hit anything on the way down. The rubber floor mat even padded my butt, but it didn't help me breathe with—I guessed—a 250-pound weight on my chest.

I froze, and so did Tane. The rest of the bar was unnaturally silent and Tane was stiff on top of me—for one beat. Our bodies aligned to put his breath in my ear, our legs wedged between each other's. And in the next beat, Tane softened slightly, and the exhale of air rushed by my ear. One might have called it a sigh.

Muscles flexed against me, pecs and abs and others I couldn't name as Tane tried to push off the ground. We both turned our heads, and Tane's eyes were wide and a smooth dark brown. He focused right on me for a moment, until two sets of hands wrapped around his biceps and hauled.

And then he was gone, Ron and Nina quick to roll Tane off me.

"Not again," Nina muttered under her breath. "Ron, help me get him upstairs. Claire, are you okay?"

I waved her off, sitting up and assessing my body. "I'm fine, I'm fine." I stood and dusted myself off, inspecting my elbows and knees. By the time I looked up again, Nina and Ron were unlocking a door in the corner I had never noticed before, Nina shouting, "Be back in a sec!" Tane was slung between them, a beefy arm over each shoulder. I raised a brow. Behind the door was a narrow staircase that led to the second floor, above the kitchen. It was very narrow—how on earth were they going to manage that?

The door slammed shut and I had to trust that Nina could handle it. My heart rate was finally starting to slow down. I'd had more than enough drunken confrontations in my life, but they were never fun.

A few customers had left in the mayhem, colorful bills tucked under empty glasses. That included the young guys, so that was one problem taken care of. The remaining bunch had decided it was a good time to leave too, so I checked the rest out, apologizing for the scene.

I kept cleaning, putting away glasses and restocking. When the door opened again, Ron stepped out.

"Aye, Claire. Nina says you can go home. I'll take care of it from here."

I nodded. "Right. Okay. I'll . . . be here tomorrow?"

I rolled my eyes inwardly at my own inflection. Ron wasn't my boss—though I had questions about who my boss was, for that matter—and my schedule, or lack thereof, wasn't up to him.

"Yup," he said, oblivious to my inner turmoil. "See you tomorrow."

—————

I stepped out of the hall bathroom at the hostel, dressed and towel-drying my hair. I'd gotten it cut a few days before my flight, going from straight black hair down my back to a shaggy pixie cut, and it was times like these that I didn't miss my long hair. Despite the late hour, the stress, and the hot shower, I was too wired to sleep. I crept down to the lounge in the hostel and took a seat.

Pulling my phone up, I squinted at the screen and did some complicated math. What time was it in Chicago? Two a.m., minus nineteen, carry the one . . .

Ugh. Time zones.

I gave up and just opened WhatsApp to message my sister, Iris, anyway. It was her problem if she didn't have do not disturb on.

Hey. You up?

Yes! How's the future?

Well, I am probably getting fired tomorrow. I lasted one whole week.

Instead of texting back, my phone vibrated and her picture popped up.

I answered and Iris screeched, "What do you mean, you're getting fired tomorrow?"

I got an instant pang of guilt. Iris lent me the money for my flight to New Zealand, and while she was certainly doing better than I was, I knew she hadn't factored in having to give her sister thousands of dollars so she could escape a stalker.

"I'll find another job," I said quickly. "I still plan on paying you back."

She huffed in my ear. "I don't *care* about that. Well, I mean, I do care," she amended. We were raised too poor not to worry about money, even —or especially—if it was loaned to family. "What happened with your job?"

I recounted the story of the dudes at the table, how the biggest one tried to get behind the bar, and how I stood my ground.

"He said, 'Don't you know who I am?' and of course I didn't. Well, it turned out," I finished, "that he's the owner of the bar. I think Nina, my boss, is his sister. So it's like . . . a family thing?"

Iris got right to the point. "He sounds like a dick."

I snorted. "Yeah, he was."

"Are you okay?" I hated the way her voice wobbled, and I knew exactly what she was thinking. The last thing I needed was more problem men in my life, and I hadn't come halfway around the world to get hurt—physically or otherwise.

"I am completely fine," I assured her.

"Really, really fine?" she needled.

"Really, really, really, really . . ." I tacked on about fifty more *really*s until Iris interrupted me, laughing.

"Okay, okay, I get it." She let her chuckle taper off and I heard a big gulp of air, my sister trying to clear her worry from her mind and move on. "I can't believe he was that drunk. Surely you tried to bat your eyelashes at him and give him your best customer-service-fuck-you smile," she teased me. I had a resting bitch face, unlike my sister, who was sunshine and rainbows. It was a miracle people let me work in the service industry.

"I called him *sir.* A lot."

She hummed.

"Where are you anyway?" I asked. "What time is it there?"

"It's seven. I'm getting ready for work," she answered me absentmindedly. Iris was an office manager, the kind who stocked supplies and helped people in the law firm she worked for, brilliant minds with sharp suits and fancy degrees who couldn't get the printer to work. I could picture her now pausing over her breakfast, tapping her chin with her finger, and could practically hear her thinking through the phone line. "He said, 'Don't you know who I am?'" she repeated.

"Yup."

"Well, let's find out who he is. What did you say his name was again?"

I sounded it out the best I could, mimicking the way Nina said it. *Tah-nay*. Then Iris asked Nina's name, and the name of the bar, but before I could spell it for her, she interrupted me. "Aha!"

"You found him already?"

"Yes, Claiiiiire! You didn't tell me he was so hot!"

"It was hard to focus on the hotness when I was being yelled at."

"I'm sending you a link to his Wikipedia page."

He has a Wikipedia page? "I'm on my phone, Iris, and I don't have a laptop."

"Put me on speaker."

I looked around, verifying that I was, in fact, alone at the late hour, before I did, clicking the link when it came through WhatsApp. My eyes skimmed the page.

Tane Taumata, international rugby player, World Cup, MVP, gold medal, career-ending injury.

"Wow." I scrolled back up more slowly, looking at the pictures. "Okay, he doesn't really look that good in person. . . ."

"Hush, I'm reading," she reprimanded me.

I smiled at my phone. Iris was always more about the details than I was, and I bet she was cataloging all this info about Tane and practically profiling him. While I waited, I scrolled back up to the "Personal life" section.

It was pretty short. There was probably more information on Wikipedia about college football stars.

Tane Taumata was born in Auckland. His father was also a former New Zealand rugby player. During his time playing professionally, Tane was often associated with musician and model Nelly Buxly, though each has denied a relationship. In 2021, he opened Haft & Hops with his sister, Nina. He currently resides in Wellington.

I clicked on one of the sources for Nelly Buxly and found a picture of her and Tane together at a black-tie event. Tane, in a perfectly tailored tux, looked trimmer and younger. Miss Buxly was heavily made-up, platinum blond, and had a bust size at least three times my small B-cups. I rolled my eyes at myself and navigated back to the previous page.

"God, I bet that was hard."

I nearly jumped out of my skin, having forgotten that Iris was on the phone with me. "What was?"

"His injury. Claire, are you reading this thing?" she asked, exasperated. "He injured his ACL. More than once."

I winced. "That's a rough one. I was looking at pictures," I said, defending myself.

Her tone got suggestive. "Looking at the pictures, huh? Why look when you can see him in person?"

"Excuse me, Miss I Have a Boyfriend." Iris had been dating Chris for almost two years and they lived together in Chicago. I had hated that Iris had moved away from our home in Boston, but eventually, when things with my ex–best friend, Devon, had gotten out of hand, I was glad she was away from it.

"Come on, Claire. Eye candy. Hello."

"Well, he doesn't look like that anymore," I insisted.

"This picture I'm looking at is, like, two years ago. He can't look that bad."

"He doesn't look bad. He's just . . . different." I swiped up and carefully typed Tane's name into the search bar and switched to image search. "First of all, he's very trim in these photos. Tane now has gotten a bit . . . soft. And squishy."

"That'll happen when you quit playing sports professionally."

"And when you drink too much," I pointed out.

Iris was quiet for a moment. "Do you think he has a drinking problem?"

"Yes," I answered without hesitation. "It's not okay to yell at people or to be sloppy drunk or have to have your sister take care of you when you can't find your way home even if it's just up a flight of stairs."

She tsked over the phone line. "Maybe he needs help."

"I spent five minutes in his presence and I know he needs help. But that's not up to me."

I couldn't read the silence on the other end of the line, but I figured Iris was probably browsing photos or reading more articles, so I did too.

"I said shirtless," she muttered a few minutes later.

"What?" I choked out while laughing.

"I'm talking to the internet. Looking for 'Tane Taumata shirtless' didn't work." I heard a huff of indignation through the phone.

"He's not your type, Iris."

"He's not your type either. Raging asshole is no one's type." There was a moment's pause. "But he's still fun to look at."

"So." I tilted my head and took on a cheery tone. "How's your boyfriend?"

I could practically hear her eyes roll from Chicago, but she allowed the change of topic anyway and launched into the latest news about Chris and his job. He wasn't my favorite person, but he seemed to make her happy. And I knew that he made more money than my sister and helped her have a good life, which had freed up some of her cash to help me.

But I also think he complained about money a lot. It stung because I already felt bad enough about it. I didn't need to also be responsible for tension in their relationship.

I listened to her talk while I flossed and brushed my teeth in the communal bathroom, finally saying goodbye as my sister, halfway around the world, got in her car to go to work.

I tiptoed into the dorm and lay down on my bed. Staring at the bunk above me, I wished I'd changed the topic of conversation away from Tane. The confrontation was all I could think about. I hadn't lied to Iris—I really was okay. Really.

But my final thoughts were that even if I wasn't going to be fired, maybe I should look for a new job anyway.

THREE

Morning brought reality. Leaving my job would be irresponsible. I needed to repay Iris and work on saving up for a plane ticket back home, as well as some basics like eating something other than canned soup and peanut butter sandwiches.

I might be fired. Or I might not.

As I turned on my phone, the still-open browser filled my screen with pictures of Tane. I gave them one more look. Then I clicked over and finally read the whole Wikipedia article—which, to be fair, wasn't that long—and went down a rabbit hole. Beyond the rugby games played on the Boston Common or back in high school, I knew very little about the sport. Except that it was a rough game.

So Tane Taumata and his sister who, so far, I adored, owned the bar together. He had drunk too much the night before and was probably going to fire me.

I tore myself away from the internet in time for my commute on the bus, and stepped into Haft & Hops fifteen minutes before my shift. Right away my eyes met Nina's and she quickly stepped over and threw her arms around me.

"Claire. I am so, so sorry about my brother."

Nina was in her mid-forties, with long dark hair that she wore in a bun on top of her head. Her hugs were good—mom hugs, soft and inviting. She had hugged me when I'd accepted the job, and even in just my first week I had learned that Nina was affectionate. She was kind of a badass, too—raising two girls by day and running a bar by night. When I'd arrived for my first shift, before the bar had opened for the day, I'd found Nina and the girls in one of the booths, Nina in the middle while she read to them. She instructed me from there, and eventually her husband, Hemi, had come in to pick the girls up and take them back home.

She patted me with a heavily tattooed arm as she pulled back. She searched my face. "You didn't get hurt, right?"

I twisted around and pointed at my butt. "Seriously, have you seen my lack of padding here?" I joked. "Next time tell your brother to land on someone else."

"Yeah, maybe one of his drinking buddies will take the fall instead," she said sourly.

"Is he okay?" I asked as she went back to restocking the fridge under the bar and I washed my hands.

"Slice lemons," she ordered, pointing at the drawer that stored the cutting boards. I obeyed, pulling out a board and knife before grabbing the fruit from the reach-in. "That thick-skulled idiot is fine. He always is."

I glanced at her out of the corner of my eye. "Does this happen often?"

"Not . . . Well, I want to say not often, but it's probably too often. My brother was a rugby player but got injured, and he just hasn't been the same since. He's been out of town this past week, so I hadn't had the chance to introduce you to him."

I stayed quiet for a moment, trying to think about how to be diplomatic, but decided, fuck it. "Can he fire me?"

"No. New Zealand laws are very strict about these kinds of things," Nina said, jaw set. "It wasn't your fault. And I know he didn't mean it." She looked at me and I kept my face neutral. "Fuck. I'm going to kill him." She slammed the fridge door shut. "Last night wasn't even his worst night. I don't know what to do."

I didn't know anything about how to deal with this scenario, but I also knew Nina wasn't looking for answers at that moment. Just a friend.

I wrapped an arm around her shoulders.

"Ooo . . ." she let out softly. "My first Claire hug."

I laughed. "What? We've hugged before."

"No, *I've* hugged *you*. There's a difference."

I wrapped my other arm around her, squeezing tight while she laughed. "Sorry my hugs are bony."

She swatted my shoulder as I let go. "It was a good hug. Don't hold out on me anymore." She laughed as she walked away to a customer flagging her down.

Later, during a lull in service, Nina was wiping down the bar and asked me what my plan was for traveling.

"What do you mean?" I asked.

"You know, you've got your visa—what's your plan to explore? Where are you going to go first?"

"Oh." I shrugged. "I don't have time to travel. I need to earn money."

Nina dramatically slapped her forehead. "Claire. You flew all the way over here and you have what, a year? You have to be excited about something! Plus, you can't work that much here. You have free time. You need to use it."

I smiled, not wanting to admit that I didn't really know much about New Zealand. "I don't have a car, so that's going to be a little tricky."

"Hm." She wrinkled her nose. "You can buy one. A lot of used cars come here from Japan, where emissions regulations are tougher on older cars. You can get one pretty cheaply."

I nibbled my lip. "I don't have the money for that."

She shot me an apologetic glance. "There are things to do around Wellington, too. Or you can make some friends in your hostel and travel with them, I'm sure. Plenty of people are driving around."

"You aren't suggesting I should"—I gasped theatrically—"make friends, are you?"

"Make friends and take advantage of them."

"Only friends with cars, of course," I bantered back.

A customer called me down to the other end of the bar and I poured them one of the craft beers on tap. Okay, so I had no money. But surely, I would be able to afford a trip sometime before my year was up. And yeah, I hadn't wanted to leave Boston, but odds were very, very good that I'd never have the opportunity to travel to New Zealand—or anywhere else on this side of the world—ever again.

I closed out the tab for the next customer and, seeing no one else demanding my immediate attention, walked back toward Nina.

"So," I said, resting a hand on the cooler next to me. "Where would you recommend that I visit?"

Nina's face lit up, and she told me to wait a minute. She scampered to the office and returned with a pad of paper and a pen. "Okay, which hostel are you staying at?"

I told her I was staying at Whakahoa and she clapped a hand over her mouth, suppressing a laugh. "What?" I asked.

"The *wh* is pronounced like an *f*." She said the name properly and I tried to repeat it. *Faka-hoa.*

I looked up at the ceiling. "So I've been saying it wrong this whole time?"

Nina nodded.

"I've been here two weeks, Nina! Two weeks! No one said anything!"

She laughed, and bent her head over the paper. "Okay, here are my favorite places." The list ended up being about twenty items long. Some of them, Nina had explained, were near impossible to get to without a car, but all of them were within a day's driving distance on the North Island and were free or very cheap.

Opportunities I'd never considered suddenly seemed possible. Maybe this could be about more than an escape.

A door opened upstairs and I heard the clomp of footsteps coming down. Nina and I glanced at each other and then at the door to Tane's place. Happy thoughts of traveling the country rushed out of my mind and I held my breath while the door creaked open.

Tane lumbered in, shoulders slumped and lips turned down in a hangover frown. He placed his forearms on the bar top and heaved himself onto a stool across from Nina. He blinked and rubbed his hands over his face and head, delaying confronting the glare Nina was giving him.

Finally he slumped down farther and met her gaze. "Sorry," he said quietly.

Nina sighed and pushed away from him, stepping over to the coffee machine to pour him a mug. "You need to be more careful, Tane."

"I know," he said, resigned.

"Somebody is going to get hurt, and your name will be tied to it and what kind of role model—"

"I know. I *know*." The last word echoed around the bar, and the few patrons we had in the early afternoon dipped into a hushed silence for a beat.

Nina placed the mug in front of him while he took a few deep breaths directly into his hands. When his palms dropped, he held Nina's gaze, and the moment held a certain sibling intimacy I was all too familiar with. Iris and I had shared that look enough times.

I tried to turn my attention elsewhere, to give Nina and Tane space, but the bar was only so big and they sat between me and the rest of the room. As Tane and Nina spoke quietly, I eyed the pass-through—the scene of the crime last night, as it was—and considered ducking through to give them more privacy.

But Nina stepped back from the bar and raised her voice. "You owe Claire an apology too."

Tane sipped from his mug and blinked at her. "Who's Claire?"

Nina gestured at me and when his eyes met mine, they widened. I cocked a hip against the bar while Tane's gaze flittered over my features.

"Did I"—he swallowed—"hit on you?"

Nina choked out a no and I narrowed my eyes. "Excuse me?"

He held his hands up. "It's a compliment."

"Like hell it is," I shot back.

"Well, then I guess it's a good thing I didn't."

"Oi!" Nina interrupted. "You wanted to go behind the bar and she—very reasonably, I might add—stopped you. You yelled some not very nice things at her and tried to force your way back before passing out."

Tane's forehead thunked against the bar and a low groan was muffled by his arms. When he sat up again, he took a fortifying gulp of coffee and looked down the bar at me. He cleared his throat. "Sorry, Claire. It was just me and my mates having a good time and . . ."

Nina crossed her arms and cleared her throat.

"Right, just . . . sorry." Tane flushed, chagrined. The corner of his mouth crinkled, an effort through the haze of a headache to look charming, I was sure. I'd bet plenty of professional athletes had the charm nailed down to get them out of all kinds of trouble when they wanted to.

Too bad for Tane I was immune to his charms already.

Nina looked at me, eyebrow raised. I wondered if she would do more poking and ear pulling if I still wasn't happy, but I relaxed my arms to my sides. "Thank you," I said stiffly. "I just want to do my job."

"Right." Tane saluted me with his mug while standing up. "You do your job and I'll stay out of your way. Fair?" He held out a hand to shake.

"Fair." I reached across the bar, fitting my hand in his and firmly shaking it. Tane glanced down, holding on to my hand a second longer than necessary.

He shook whatever thoughts he had—probably hangover-related with hopefully a dash of embarrassment—and came around the bar to refill his coffee. Nina moved aside to let him through. "We good, bro?" she said.

"We're good." Tane poured his coffee and said something in Māori that had Nina rolling her eyes and slapping his shoulder. He grinned at her and walked back around to the door upstairs. Before he disappeared, he met my eyes and raised his mug at me again.

Nina's face was lit up with warmth and affection for her brother, and I tried to swallow down the homesickness that rose inside me. My job was safe, and that was what mattered.

FOUR

A sense of relief washed over me as my bank confirmed the transfer. One hundred dollars sent to Iris Bailey.

It was a pittance. A drop in the bucket of what I owed her, but just the fact that I was starting to pay her back was a big deal to me. I shouldn't have to depend on my little sister for money.

The next deposit would be a thousand dollars, I vowed.

New Zealand hadn't been my first choice for places to go, simply because I hadn't wanted to go anywhere. I loved Boston. It was a perfectly sized city, with nice public transportation and a great bar scene, and it had been my home for my entire life. In fact, this was my first trip away from the US, and honestly, I hadn't wanted to go.

But I'd felt like I'd had no choice.

Running out of options and beginning to be truly scared, I had sat down one early morning after the bar I worked at had closed. I had little money, since living in Boston was so fucking expensive, and because I'd changed jobs three times in the past year, my reputation and bank account had taken a hit.

As long as Devon was in Boston, I wanted to be as far away as possible. So I searched the internet. How far could I get?

Turned out the farthest point on the other side of the world was a Podunk little town in Australia called Augusta, but a quick search said they had limited bartending options for their population of one thousand. I was picturing it like the Wild, Wild West with me rolling up in my short hair, nose piercing, black boots, and nerdy T-shirts, and someone with a really bizarre accent telling me they "don't take too kindly to strangers around these parts, mate."

But then I searched "how to move to Australia" and, lo and behold, there was a visa perfect for me—anyone under thirty could come to the country for a year and work. And oh, New Zealand had one too.

I started emailing bars, researching walkable cities. All my money wasn't enough—I had to prove solvency for the application and that I had the funds to get myself in and out of New Zealand. I had called up Iris, desperate.

"He was here again," I started.

"Did you call the police?" Iris asked, immediately on alert.

"My manager wouldn't let me. He said that twice was one too many times, and it didn't look good for the bar to have police around all the time."

"Claire, you've got to go."

At the time, she just meant leaving the job. I sucked a lungful of air in and I asked Iris, my little sister with a better job and home life than I had, if I could borrow thousands of dollars.

Of course she had said yes.

I still felt shitty about it.

But here I was, halfway around the world. After my plane ticket, my application, and proof of funds, I couldn't afford a car. I'd hunted online for jobs in the bigger cities.

And Haft & Hops had been perfect.

Okay, maybe not perfect. But something close. It was far away from Boston and they'd offered me a job. That, I could work with.

Haft & Hops wasn't just a bar, though. It had been a winery on the outskirts of Wellington, but as the city had grown, the area had been developed into suburbs. But it had been converted into a bar and an axe-throwing range. It seemed the craze had made it over to New Zealand, too. I'd seen a few around Boston, but had never been.

I had a place to work, a cheap hostel downtown, and a reliable bus route between the two. And Devon didn't know where I was.

It was heaven.

And after my conversation the night prior with Nina, her excitement had invigorated me. I felt the thrill of wanderlust creeping through my body, the adrenaline building the more I saw all that New Zealand had to offer.

By the time I needed to get dressed and catch the bus to go to work, my head was full of ideas.

———

That drunken scene with Tane didn't happen again, but over the next three weeks I learned that his routine was reliable. Most nights he came down, drinking with a mix of guys in one of the back booths.

On those nights, Tane was loud, surrounded by the same guys, doing the same cheers and chants. Over time, I picked up tidbits here and there of their lives. They all loved rugby, and Tane was worshipped for being a superstar. They were around on busy nights, adding to the cacophony in the room.

Sometimes I'd catch a certain noise that would stand out to my ear and I'd look up and my eyes would meet Tane's.

But Tane still drank a lot. Nina ran defense when he got too drunk, scattering the group with the usual threats and then getting Tane upstairs. If he was too wasted or the bar was still too busy for a bouncer to leave his shift, Tane was put in the office to sleep it off.

My coworkers mostly ignored him, so I did too.

There were some nights, though, when Tane's crew wasn't around. They were the quieter nights, when the ones who did show up mumbled about kids and wives as they paid and left early.

And soon it would be just Tane in the back, drinking alone. He drew my eye even more on those nights.

"How about another round, love?" the guy three seats down called out to me, pulling my attention away from Tane. The man, easily in his sixties, had been drinking for a few hours, steadily nursing whiskeys.

He wasn't drunk, at least not that I thought, but a little voice whispered in the back of my mind that I should start encouraging him to move on.

A bartender's intuition.

I smiled at him and pulled out a clean glass. "You got it."

"The good stuff." He gestured up and behind me at the top shelf as I filled the glass with ice.

"Sure." I turned around, reaching up to grab the bottle, and then spun back to the bar. He didn't even try to hide that he had been staring at my ass, and his gaze barely shifted to the glass while I poured and then put the bottle back.

"There you are, sir."

"Thank you."

I took two paces away before he spoke again. "Where are you from in the States?"

Stopping at the computer, I called out over my shoulder, "Boston." I added the drink to his tab as he told me about his visit to Boston twenty-odd years ago.

"What's a girl like you doing here? Shouldn't you be down in Queenstown bungee jumping with all the kids your age?" He chuckled to himself. "Or maybe you aren't into hanging out with people your own age?" He winked.

I laughed to cover up my discomfort, and kept my answer bland. "Oh, I hang out with all types." I moved farther away down the bar, but he kept talking to me anyway.

"I knew a girl like you once," he said, just as I was getting too far away to be politely conversing at a normal volume. I was familiar with this move. The goal was to keep me near, focus my attention on him, start to make me uncomfortable.

The worst guys always tried it when the bar was quiet, when I didn't have other customers to tend to. When ignoring them bordered on rude.

I didn't go closer, but I didn't move away, either. Instead I busied myself straightening things that didn't really need straightening, wiping things down that didn't really need wiping.

"She was beautiful, just like you," he continued.

I couldn't help the way hearing that made my skin crawl, my shoulders climb up to my ears. All I could think of were Devon's words: *But you're so beautiful.* As if that were the only thing that mattered, as if it were all he could see about me, even after years of being best friends and growing up together.

As the guy droned on about some "bird" he knew back in the seventies when "women were much less uptight," I glanced over at Ron, who was on his phone.

Seemed like Ron was going to be useless once again.

The empty glass clinked as it was dropped on the bar. "Another, love."

I raised an eyebrow at the speed at which the last drink had gone down. "Certainly," I said, snatching up the glass.

This time I gave the glass a little "prewash," leaving some water in it before I tossed in ice and spun away. I kept my body between the glass and the customer while I poured, watering down his whiskey.

When I turned back, I jumped. Tane stood next to the man, palms on the bar and empty glass in front of him. He was close to the older guy—too close, his arm clearly in the guy's space, so close that I felt a sense of satisfaction over the discomfort on the man's face.

"Another shout, Claire. And this one's tab." He cocked his head at the guy.

"Wh-what?" the older man sputtered. "I'm not done yet."

"Well, I think you are."

The man grabbed his drink like that would prevent Tane from kicking him out of the bar. "We've just been having a chat."

"You're not having a chat. You know it, I know it, even Ron at the door knows it"—Tane raised his voice—"even if he's a right muppet about it." Tane turned back to the guy while Ron lumbered to his feet. I tossed the receipt onto the bar.

He sneered. "Your generation thinks you're so careful. You didn't even ask her! What sexist bollocks."

Tane turned to me. "Want him gone?"

"Yup." I popped the *p*.

"Right, that's enough of that."

Amid much protesting and a few choice words, Ron and Tane managed to get the customer out the door. They stayed outside for longer than I expected, but the big carved wood doors kept me from seeing what was happening. With visions of violence and injuries, I slipped under the bar and gently pushed the door open.

Tane and Ron had their backs turned to me. The creep was nowhere to be seen, but Tane stood with his brow furrowed, his tongue sharp with forced patience.

". . . need to be more proactive about this stuff. Just cause your mum's friends with Nina, doesn't mean you get to slack off. Nina will fire you if she has to."

"If he'd hurt Claire, I could have taken care of him," Ron said, a defensive note in his voice.

"I have no doubt Claire, or any of the other bartenders, could take care of themselves. But that's not their job; it's yours. I'm half pissed and I could tell it was time to move him on. You gotta pay attention, bro."

I pulled back, letting the door close without calling attention to myself, and retreated to the bar. Tane's glass sat by the taps, a pool of condensation underneath.

A few minutes later, Tane and Ron strode back in, Ron taking his seat and Tane making for the door to his apartment.

"Tane?"

He stalled mid-stride. "Yeah?"

I glanced around at the remaining customers, wondering what had really made me call out and stop him. My eyes fell to his glass again. "You want that beer?"

He stared at it for a moment, as if forgetting what it was. "Nah, ta though."

"A water?"

A brow quirked in what might have been amusement. "Make it an L&P."

He straddled the barstool while I poured him a glass of the carbonated lemony beverage touted on the bottle to be "World Famous in New Zealand." I most often served it with Southern Comfort, a combination I found amusing.

"Thanks for that." I tilted my chin up toward the door.

"Yeah, no worries."

Tane sat for a few minutes in silence while I puttered around, wondering why I'd offered him a drink in his own bar. If he wanted his own damn drink, he could get his own damn drink.

"You've had a pretty eventful first month," he said. "It's not usually like this, I swear. Nina's pretty good at keeping the riffraff out."

"Ah, I don't know . . ." I drawled, feeling a little cheeky. "She keeps you around."

A big palm went to his chest, mockingly covering his wounded heart. His face didn't change, though, and I thought he might be even better at the deadpan delivery than I was.

I suppressed my smile.

"She's worth keeping around, eh." He traced the condensation on the glass and I thought I saw the ghost of a smile, the affection for his sister slipping out.

"Have you always been this close?" I asked.

Tane ran a hand over the cropped hair on his scalp. "We weren't when I was playing, you know, always on tour with the team and I wasn't around much. Missed her kids being born and stuff like that. But after I retired, she started to get real bossy." At that, he smirked.

"Nina, bossy? Never."

"Yeah, you know, most of the players fuck around for a while, but Nina sat me down and said, 'I want a bar and you're going to buy me one.'"

His smirk slid into a full-on grin and I laughed. A couple came up to close their tab and I returned to Tane a few minutes later with the patrons' empty glasses. I submerged one glass with my right hand and began to give it a good scrubbing.

"I looked you up online back when we first met. I don't know much about rugby except that it's some pretty tough guys playing. Did you retire because of your injury?"

My tone was teasing, but when I looked up, Tane's jaw was set, his face hard. Any signs of humor were gone again. He brought his glass up to his lips and drained it. "Well, I think I'll head upstairs now. Remember to give Ron a shout sooner if you need to."

"Wait, Tane, I was just asking . . ."

He stood up, eyes flashing. "It's just your curiosity, eh? Never mind it ended my career, took away my friends, killed a family legacy, and still gives me pain some days. But, hey, I'm a tough guy, right?" I'd hit a nerve, and Tane fiddled with it like an aching tooth.

"Tane—"

"Nah, don't worry about it, Claire. See you next time." Tane stomped up the stairs, leaving me bouncing off the waves and unmoored in his wake.

———

My bartending job was less complicated than I wanted it to be. I loved cocktails, but sticking with the old-winery theme, the bar served mainly beer and wine. The cocktail menu was clunky and full of the same tired drinks gracing most menus. It baffled me. Haft & Hops was classy, upscale, even, and the menu was doing it a disservice. Yes, the wines fit the theme, with grapes growing on trellises on the back lawn between the lanes of targets. The menu worked well with it too: crudités and cheese platters and fancy finger foods.

But Haft & Hops did a lot of business with tourists during the week, and bachelor and bachelorette parties—hen and stag parties—on the weekends. A revamp of their cocktail menu would *slay*.

As part of the visa rules, I could only work at one place for six months. My reputation back in Boston was ruined, but here was a clean slate. Halfway through my visit, I would have to leave Haft & Hops, but I would still be paying off Iris and searching for a second job.

I wanted to be invaluable to Nina. I wanted a golden recommendation. I wanted to keep my head down, work hard, and save money.

And maybe, just maybe, I'd get to see a little bit of the country.

Two weeks after Tane had kicked the customer out for me, I confidently made one of my favorite drinks at the end of my lunch shift, a gin fizz with egg whites, torched candied orange slices and rosemary, and carried it back to Nina's office.

"Knock, knock," I said as Nina looked up.

"What's this?" she said, leaning away from the desk.

"I made you a drink to try." I carefully placed it in front of her, mindful not to spill or let the garnish, the orange skewered with rosemary, fall out.

"Wow, it's pretty." She leaned over and sniffed, then gave me some side-eye. "This is way fancier than what we serve."

Carefully, she picked up the glass and sipped. It was in a martini glass, though a coupe would have been better. Haft & Hops lacked some of the barware I thought they could use.

Nina's eyes popped open. "Wooooowwwwwww. What's your secret? It's so . . ." Her eyes unfocused as she was thinking and tasting.

I told her about the ingredients and my techniques, probably going into too many details about the process of infusing the simple syrup. Nina owned her own bar; she wasn't stupid. But my enthusiasm got out of hand.

"It's fresh," she said, after a second sip. "Tastes like summer."

"We can go seasonal with the drinks. But something crafted like this would sell well here. It fits the atmosphere," I pointed out. "What do you think?" I tipped my chin at her near-empty glass. "If you want, I can get some more suggestions together, change up the menu a little bit. Or just do a daily special."

Nina placed the drink back down on the desk and spun toward me fully. "Is this what you did back in the States? These kinds of cocktails?"

"Sometimes. The bars I worked at weren't always the best. I worked at a lot of dives, but sometimes they were hangouts for the staff who worked at nicer places and were looking for a cheap drink. I served lots of basic drinks like you have on the menu. But Haft & Hops has so much potential. It's fancy and really pretty inside."

Nina looked thoughtful. "You made this with things we already had in stock?"

"Not the orange, because that's been candied. But everything else, yes. I made a flavored simple syrup, which is a lot of work when you can just order them. But everything else you already had."

I swear something flashed behind her eyes. Anticipation? Mischief?

"I would love to offer some upscale cocktails," she began. My lips curled with premature excitement. "But we have to run it by Tane."

My smile fell. "Wait, why?" It came out sharper than I'd intended. I softened my words. "No offense, but he's not around that much. Do you really need his input on this?"

"Claire," Nina said in gentle reprimand. "He's my partner."

"Yeah, well . . . I may have put my foot in my mouth with him." I winced. Tane had been avoiding me. "I think he's a bit . . . mad at me."

"Do you deserve it?" she asked, amused.

"I asked about his injury."

"Ah," she said, leaning back in her chair. "That would do it."

"Yeah . . . I didn't realize I was poking a nerve. But he's also not helping," I added, feeling the need to defend myself a little bit.

"It's still sore. Give it time and talk about something else."

"Tane did tell me he bought you the bar."

At that, she frowned. "Yes, well, I thought it would do him some good to have a place to belong after rugby. I'm not so sure anymore if that was a good idea."

I wasn't one to deliver fake platitudes, so I searched my brain for something positive to say. "He seems to have a lot of friends."

"Well, when you're a famous rugby player in your own right and then the son of another famous one on top of that, you tend to make friends easily in New Zealand. Some of those friends I wish would be a better influence. But I think the best ones are still out playing rugby.”

“Right, well, I’ll find something else to talk to him about, then. Any advice?”

She scrunched up her nose, what I thought might be bitterness infusing her voice. “Just rugby and beer.”

Rugby was a big goose egg for me, but I could talk about beer.

“I’m sure you’ll find some common ground. Talk to him about the cocktails.” She nodded at the empty glass. “You’ll win him over,” she reassured me. “Your drink *is* that good.”

FIVE

When I got back to my hostel after my shift, my day got worse. I had booked a dorm bunk, which sounded fun at the time. Hey, I never went to college. This could be like college, right?

Maybe it was. Maybe in college there was always someone getting up early—the ones working agriculture—and someone always coming in late—me and all the other hospitality people. Maybe there was always someone who smelled bad enough to stink up the whole room or someone who spilled an unknown substance on the floor or someone who for some explicable reason decided that *my* bed was the perfect place to put their day-old dirty plate of curry when there was a rule about no food allowed in the dorm room and you had to do your own dishes and clean up after yourself.

So far, my seven weeks of dorm life had been a huge disappointment, and I was worn thin.

"Goddamn it," I muttered as I dropped my clean T-shirt on the wet floor of the bathroom for the seventh time that week. I'd learned the first day that it was a no-no to walk around with a towel on, even if you forgot something from the dorm room. But seriously, couldn't the shower stall have more than one hook? I had to balance my clean clothes, dirty clothes, and a towel.

The towel was a whole other drama. No, I didn't know to bring my own towel, thank you very much. I'd had to rent one the first few nights. Now, after weeks of watching people, there was an additional shopping list of things I needed to get to make my stay more comfortable. People carried their toiletries around in little bags they could hang in the shower and had cheap flip-flops they *only* wore in the shower stalls.

Dressed in—relatively—clean clothes, I returned to the dorm room. Since I'd worked the day shift, it was late afternoon and the hostel was buzzing. Actually buzzing—oh wait, that was my phone.

"Good evening," Iris said cheerfully.

I grumbled something that might have been polite but probably was not.

"Did I wake you up? Wait a minute . . . what time is it?"

"No, you didn't wake me," I told her. "I'm off work and just out of the shower."

"Why are you so grumpy, then?"

"I'm always grumpy."

"You know I love your bitchy face, but you sound . . . not yourself. Did the owner yell at you again?"

"No," I admitted. "But I did talk to Nina today about the cocktail menu. She liked the drink I made."

Iris snorted. "Of course she did. It was delicious."

"You can taste it from there?" My voice carried too much snark in it and I cringed.

"Claire, what's going on?"

I dropped the attitude and sighed, leaning my head against the bunk above my bed. "I think I bit off more than I can chew here. What was I thinking?"

"Babe, give me specifics. What are the *actual* things that are wrong?"

I told her about the towels, the roommates, the loudness, the wet side of my T-shirt where it had touched the grimy floor that never seemed clean or dry.

"It sounds like you have a hostel problem."

"I didn't realize living in a hostel had such a learning curve. People know what they need and how to pack it and I had to go buy a towel the other day because renting one was ridiculous and, apparently, I didn't buy the right one. You know how I like the super-big ones that actually cover my ass? But everyone owns these special thin ones that dry fast and fold up super small. How was I supposed to know that was a thing?"

There were typing noises in the background of the call.

"Where are you?" I asked her.

"At home, getting ready for bed. Chris is working late so I thought I'd call you. Now, let's see. What's the name of the place you're staying at?"

I told her the name of the hostel and she pulled up the website.

"Are you paying fifteen dollars a day?" Iris shrieked. "How do they even make money off of that?"

"Well, no, I'm paying a little bit more than that."

"Are you aware this place is rated four-point-five—"

"That well?"

"—out of ten on Hostelworld?"

"Um, well, no. I just googled hostels."

"Claire." Iris took a deep breath in and then out. "Please, for the love of Pete, spend an extra twenty dollars and get yourself a better hostel."

I picked a tiny fluff ball of lint off my sheets. "Okay," I sulked.

"What? Okay? Did my sister just agree to something without an argument? It's worse than you're telling me, isn't it?"

"No, it's not," I quickly assured her. "I just . . . I don't know, I feel like I hate other people right now."

"Maybe don't tell your boss that one."

I rolled my eyes.

"Okay, well, I'm booking you into a new hostel."

"Oh no," I deadpanned. "Iris. Stop."

"Har, har. I'm doing this because I love you."

"I will pay you back. Add it to my tab."

Iris mumbled something, half listening to me while she typed away. A minute later my phone buzzed against my face with a new email coming in. "It's a fifteen-minute walk away. Go pack your things and get your ass in gear."

"Thank you, Iris," I said quietly.

"You are welcome. I am so proud of you and how brave you are to just pack up and take off. Yes, there are road bumps, but you're a badass bitch who can tackle them. You just need the right environment."

"Speaking of, how's your environment?"

Iris sighed. "Donald asked me to send a fax again. A *fax*, Claire." Donald was her boss, an old-school lawyer who was too stuck in his ways to realize what a gem he had in my sister. "He also had a meeting with one of the families we're working with pro bono, a couple whose English isn't great, and because I wasn't there to translate, there was a miscommunication, and . . ." She trailed off with another big sigh.

Iris had studied Spanish and she hoped to teach it in high schools. But the move with Chris had meant she needed to be certified in Illinois, and she hadn't been able to find a teaching job aside from substituting. And it all circled back to the pay again. Chris was adamant that they keep separate finances, so Iris couldn't afford a substitute's pay and bailing out her sister and getting a master's, which was her dream.

"When I pay you back, you should put that into starting classes for your master's," I said.

"I don't know. I'm having a hard time paying for things here. Chicago's more expensive than I thought it would be."

I ignored the comment I could make about keeping up with Chris's lifestyle. "You deserve the job you want, Iris. And you would be a great teacher. Those high school twerps would be lucky to have you teaching them."

"Aw, thanks, babe." It broke my heart a little that I could hear the joy in Iris's voice that even thinking about teaching brought her.

Iris said she needed to go to sleep, so we said goodbye, leaving me free to pack. When I had arrived in New Zealand, I had a backpack and a small duffle bag. But since then I'd had to buy toiletries and a giant fluffy towel and my work uniform, and none of those new things fit into my bags.

I must have spent too long staring at my stuff laid out on the bed. A guy on the bunk across from me offered his opinion.

"Put the heavier stuff in your backpack so it's easier to carry. And get a plastic laundry bag from reception to bundle up your clothes."

I saluted my hostel mentor and returned a few minutes later with two bags. With everything packed up, I waddled down to the front desk and checked out. I turned right outside the hostel doors and walked down toward the waterfront.

With my backpack on, the duffle bag slung around my chest, and a trash bag in either hand, I looked like I was homeless. I had to stop at the corners, set my stuff down, and whip out my phone, memorizing the next set of directions, but it worked.

Until one of the bags started to rip and make a slow descent as the weight in my hands succumbed to gravity. And then the other bag tried to slip out of my sweaty hands.

I pulled the ripping one against my body and tried to waddle faster. I took a right turn down a street that was much busier than the others—Lambton Quay, according to my phone. As I was checking the map again, someone bumped into my duffle bag, sending it rocketing off my shoulder. Everything slipped.

Yup. My dirty laundry was now all over the sidewalk. Black thongs and stinky sports bras and pants that smelled like I was an alcoholic.

And here was the thing about Wellington. It was *windy*. All the time, it felt like. And some of my clothes, the lighter stuff that could catch some air, started to blow around.

There went one of my thongs, flying underneath a passing car.

I dropped the stuff that was still contained in the other bag and chased after my things. But, in a move that would never happen in Boston, people stopped to help. I wasn't sure if I was thankful or mortified. Strangers were handing me my underwear as I put my stuff to the side in a pile blocked from the wind.

"Thank you so much," I said, crouching down as the last sock got added to the pile, and the stranger, a kid who was probably fifteen years old, dusted his hands off and walked away.

"Claire?" a deep, tentative voice asked.

I looked up. Tane stood at the open door of a black sedan stopped in the street, his brow furrowed as he took in the scene. He was dressed up, much more than he would be at the bar, in slacks and a collared shirt, sleeves rolled up to his elbows.

He bent down and said something to the driver before stepping away and closing the door. He jogged the few steps over to me and came to a stop, taking in the mess and picking up the last errant pair of panties from the street. He frowned at it, but handed it to me with concern in his eyes rather than disgust.

We eyed each other warily as people stepped around us, loud groups of friends going out to dinner or people going home from work.

"Your bundle didn't work, eh?" he asked, nudging a sock.

"The trash bag wasn't even my idea." When he looked over at me, I explained further. "I'm kind of new to the hostel scene."

"Are you"—his brow furrowed again, his gaze taking in my things—"in between hostels?"

"Yeah," I said, reaching over and untying the mouth of the other bag. My dignity was too far gone today. I had no fucks left to give. "Maybe I can fit my dirty clothes in with my clean?"

"Hey, wait, what about—" He paused before reaching into the bag. "May I?"

I made a *sure* gesture and he reached in and pulled out the giant fluffy towel. He spread it out on the ground and started to shovel my clothes into the center. Once we had a somewhat organized pile, he brought the corners together, making a bundle that he then hefted up easily. Even though he clearly wasn't in peak physical condition anymore, he was much better equipped in the muscle department than I was to just deadlift thirty pounds of laundry.

I tried not to stare as the muscles of his forearm flexed and rolled. The pictures Iris and I had ogled online showed muscular and veined arms. I thought I liked this better—dark hair over tawny skin with just enough definition to see the strength behind it.

"Where to?"

"You really don't have to do this. I can manage."

Tane gave me some solid side-eye, the crease deepening between his black eyebrows. Didn't blame him for his doubt.

"Okay, fine." I gave him the name of the hostel and we started off down the street. I hugged the intact bag to my chest, wrapping my arms underneath the weight to try to prevent a second laundry kerfuffle.

"Which hostel *were* you in?"

He grimaced when I gave him the name. "It's good you're moving. This one's better. Were you in the dorms?"

"Yeah," I said, defensiveness creeping in, "but I have a private room now."

Tane said something not in English—I assumed Māori—but it had the edge of a curse word. "I'm surprised you still have this much stuff. It's a miracle it didn't get stolen."

"Hey, don't be a snob. We aren't all ex-superstars."

"It's just common safety. And comfort. And obviously I'm right; otherwise, you wouldn't be moving," he said, looking smug—and correct.

I remembered he was my boss and bit my tongue before I said something even more argumentative. We trudged along in silence.

"Are you meeting some friends for dinner or something?" I asked. It was interesting that we'd run into each other, but Wellington wasn't that big and this was a busy part of town. Tane was being nice enough to help; the least I could do was carry a conversation.

"A friend," he said. "She's waiting for me at the restaurant."

"Oh, well, thanks. For making her wait, I mean. I'm not necessarily sure you want to tell her you were late because you were picking up my, uh, unmentionables?"

That made Tane chuckle, and for a moment I smiled too. "I'll be sure to wash my hands first."

The smile dropped off my face. The thought of my eau-de-laundry stink all over Tane's hands made me want to curl up and die of mortification.

Two more blocks to go. I suppose I could bring up the cocktails I wanted to do for the bar, but there was a big difference between hearing about an idea for a new cocktail menu versus tasting the new cocktails.

Tane pointed out a fast-food shop on the corner. "This kebab place is really good."

"Maybe I'll check it out for dinner."

More silence. *Awkward*.

We reached my new digs and Tane opened the glass door for me, cold air rushing out. It didn't get as miserably hot here as it did in Boston in the summer, but with almost everything I owned weighing me down, I was sweating.

"Thanks, you can just put it there." I pointed to a chair.

Tane rested the bundle on the chair but didn't release it completely, which was a good thing, I guess. The chair was small, the pile large, and there were enough eyes in the lobby that I didn't want my underwear on display again.

I checked in and got my room card. A single room, shared bathroom. Tane walked behind me as I followed the receptionist's directions up the stairs and down the hallway. The door swung open to a clean, bright modern bedroom. *Oh, thank God.*

"Set it down on the bed." I gestured and Tane obeyed my instructions. The pile of laundry collapsed and a thong hit the floor of my new room. Oops.

"It's better than your last place, yeah?" Tane—thankfully ignoring my embarrassment—strode to the window, checking out the view. No, wait. Checking out the windows.

"I think I'll be fine since I'm on the second floor," I said, amused.

"Do you have brothers?" Tane asked.

"No, just one sister. Why?"

He shrugged. "It's the way I'd want someone to treat my sister or . . ." He trailed off, thinking. "Employee," he finished.

"I'm telling Nina you don't think she can handle herself."

And then Tane grinned. Wow. The pictures of him smiling and laughing that Iris and I had scoped out online had nothing on real-life Tane.

I must have been staring, because Tane wiped the smile off his face and cleared his throat. "Okay, well." He hooked a thumb over his shoulder. "I better go meet my friend."

Something in the way he said it made it sound a little special. Like it was a girlfriend. Or a hookup? Or maybe I was reading too much into it.

"Thanks again," I said as Tane stepped out into the hallway.

"You're welcome. See ya back at the bar."

And with that, Tane walked off to his hot date, and I was left with a pile of smelly laundry. At least I had kebabs in my future.

————

Having my own room was so much better. After laundry was done, dinner was eaten, and all my things were put away, I took a selfie in the doorway of my room and sent it to Iris.

And then I flopped face-first onto my bed. The new hostel was clean—really clean—and the privacy was like a long-lost friend. There were so many things I couldn't do in a dorm room, like call my sister or change clothes or masturbate.

After a few weeks without, I was definitely horny. While I was not opposed to hookups, and thoroughly enjoyed the one-night stand philosophy, an opportunity hadn't arisen yet. Most of the people I'd met in my last hostel had been coupled up or were also staying in the dorm room, and the guys who hit on me at the bar were often locals—or creeps. I didn't want to sleep with someone who was going to come around to the bar over and over again.

Packing light meant I had only a small bullet vibrator with me. I had packed a dildo in my luggage at first, but the night before I left, I had a nightmare about customs searching my bag and pulling it out for everyone to see. Though I much preferred penetration, with enough pressure and concentration, the bullet would do.

I crawled into bed and reacquainted myself with my compact but powerful new best friend in my very clean, very private room.

SIX

Thanks to the Christmas holiday, the bar was closed for a few days, but then we were slammed with New Year's and it was two weeks before I got a chance to corner Tane.

It was weird having Christmas in the summer, but my new hostel was full of activities for the guests, including a secret Santa gift exchange and a big family-style meal. That, combined with a very long video chat with Iris, rebooted my batteries enough to tackle the business of New Year's.

I was at the tail end of a lunch shift and wrapping up the day before it got too busy again. Tane was behind the bar, sober—for now—and I wasn't too busy filling drink orders to talk with him.

This is a good idea, I thought, giving myself a pep talk. *Tane's a smart business guy, Nina's on board. The worst he can do is say no. And even if he does, I'll just try again.*

"Hi. Uh, Tane." Butterflies tickled my belly, but I tamped them down.

"Ah, right," he said, stepping back from the taps. "Must ask permission before pouring a beer in my own bar."

Butterflies combusted.

"That is *not* what I was going to say! You can pour your own damn beer."

He held an empty glass out to me, wiggling both it and his eyebrows. "Why would I when it's your job?"

"The job your sister hired me to do," I snapped back.

He raised one eyebrow now, infuriatingly calm. "Exactly."

Argh. "It's fine—you can pour your own drink."

"No, no," Tane said, a hint of teasing slipping into his voice. He strode off down the bar and around to the other side, plopping onto the seat in front of me. "We can do this proper-like. You can treat me like a customer."

I rolled my eyes. "I didn't know you were the owner then."

He waved the glass at me again and I took it with a huff. Tane's lips quirked up before he suppressed his amusement, and I attempted to repress my smile too. Tilting the glass to the side, I pulled the lever on the draft to pour the locally brewed pale ale. I presented the glass with a flourish and the perfect amount of head on the beer.

"Your drink, *sir*."

Tane smirked and accepted the pint from me. He sipped and carefully turned, walking toward his buddies in the back.

"Wait," I called out. He paused and turned back, looking quizzically at me. "I have some ideas for the cocktail menu."

He frowned. "What about the cocktail menu?"

"Well, it's, like . . . gin and tonics and sidecars, and like . . . really classic cocktails. They're fine, but you could do so much more with the menu."

"What did you have in mind?" He tilted his head, curious, which I took as a good sign.

"I made this drink for Nina, a gin fizz with candied oranges, and she loved it. Let me make you one, and if you like it, we can incorporate it into the menu. With some other ideas I have, of course. You've got craft beers and local wines —why not craft cocktails?"

Tane shook his head before I was even finished. "It's too much money and too much work to stock the complicated ingredients. I like the menu we have now." He lifted his pint in a toast. "I like my beers."

"Right, but you've got lots of bachelorette—I mean, hen dos—that come in. These cocktails would sell crazy well with them, and you can charge a lot more for that section of the menu."

"But then you'd be leaving at the end of your six months, right? Who's going to make the cocktails then?"

"They aren't hard to make. It's a bit trickier to come up with them in the first place. But if we create a seasonal menu that you can rotate out, you'll be good for at least a year."

He shook his head again. "Too much work, Claire. And there's not enough market for it here." Tane ended the conversation by walking away.

"Yes, there is," I said under my breath. Sure, the clientele right now was Tane and a bunch of his rugby buddies. But ladies lunched during the week, tourists drank out back, and yeah, the weekends were full of all kinds of people.

Tane arrived at the back booth and his buddies made room for him. Each and every one of them had a beer—some craft, some popular imported brands. I chewed my lip, thinking about how I could convince a big, burly rugby player to pick up a bright pink cocktail and give it a try.

———

For the next week, Tane was only around when I was busy, but I made the decision to invest in myself. I took some of my hard-earned money and bought the ingredients I needed. I was sure that once he got a taste, it would be worth the investment. The supplies were shelf-stable, so I crossed my fingers that I would have some downtime with Tane around to mix the drinks.

I could have shrugged and given up. After all, it was Tane and Nina's bar, and their decision to make. But I was right. I *knew* I was right, that these drinks would sell, and Nina deserved that. I didn't want Tane and his beers to stand between more success for her.

Finally, on a Tuesday night, it was quiet. Well, quiet except for the rugby boys in the back, but the weather had been crappy all day, so there were no customers outside and the inside was unusually quiet.

There were six of them, so I cracked eggs, shook my concoctions, and toasted the tops. I carefully placed the drinks on a tray and carried it over to the booth. One of the guys elbowed another and soon they were no longer listening to Tane but watching me as I set the tray down on the edge of the table. Five sets of eyes watched me with interest. One of them nudged Tane.

"Claire," Tane said, exasperation coloring his voice. "I said no. It's a waste of our stock."

"It's not a waste if you drink them," I said evenly, placing a martini glass in front of each burly man. "And I paid for most of it myself. Worst case, you don't like them. Fine, then I'll be back in ten minutes to collect the glasses and dump them out. But if you do like them . . . then maybe I'll come back and all the glasses will be empty." I cocked my hip and lifted the empty tray over one shoulder. I put on my most dazzling, fakest smile ever and winked at Tane. "Enjoy your drink, sir."

As I put the tray away and settled back behind the bar, the front doors opened and a group of four came in, shaking off wet raincoats and laughing before settling in at the bar. It was more than ten minutes before I got back to the booth with the empty tray, but I did it with extra swagger and smugness.

"My, my, you boys must have been parched." The glasses were empty, save the candied orange slices. "You can eat the oranges if you want."

One of the younger guys, with blond hair and tattoos on his knuckles, picked the slice up experimentally and took a nibble.

He hummed as he took a bite. "Chewy."

Soon all the guys were picking up their oranges delicately with their thumbs and forefingers, the thin slices nearly disappearing between their thick, sporty fingers.

I leaned a hand on the table. "What do you think? You want another?"

Young Guy raised his hand like he was in school.

An older guy with a beer gut, his black hair streaked with gray, lifted a finger. "Can you make one this weekend when I bring my wife in?"

I winked at him. "You betcha."

Tane grumbled under his breath.

"I'm sorry, what was that, *sir*?"

"Fine. Yes. You can try a drink special this weekend."

A smile broke out on my face, excitement fluttering in my stomach.

Older Guy perked up and gave me a thumbs-up.

———

I'd been working hard during my two months at the bar, and things had shifted a little between Tane and me. He was still quiet and liked to give me a hard time, constantly making me pour his beers. It should have annoyed me, but he clearly found it amusing, so I rolled my eyes and poured him a beer and said, "Here you are, *sir*." Sometimes, instead of drinking in the back, he sat at the bar.

The one thing was that Iris was starting to worry me. While she wasn't putting pressure on me, we'd had a phone call and I'd heard Chris in the background. She kept shushing him, but my gut told me it was about the money I'd borrowed. I tried to shake it off and focus.

The drink special was happening Saturday, and I came in early to line up the drinks. I premade the simple syrup, stocked up on candied orange slices, checked the torches, and redrew the special on the chalkboard about fifty times until it didn't look like a two-year-old had written it.

"It looks great," Marissa, one of the bartenders who worked with me often, assured me. We had already gone over the recipe together, and she'd been enthusiastic and patient. Younger than I was, Marissa was a Kiwi and had been working at the bar for almost a year. "Tane and Nina are going to love it."

As customers started filing in, Marissa and I told everyone about the cocktail. Some locals grumbled, raising eyebrows at the chalkboard and asking what the new beers were instead, but on a Saturday night the bar slanted toward the younger or tourist crowd anyway. We were soon running low on the ingredients.

Nina was busy outside, keeping an eye on customers interested in a round of axe-throwing before they drank. But at one point, Marissa nudged me and lifted her chin toward the back, where Nina was standing in the open door, waiting to catch my eye. She gave me a big grin and a double thumbs-up.

"That's one happy owner down," Marissa remarked as she passed me to head back to the storage room for a resupply. "Now, where's the other one?"

I wondered that too. Some of Tane's friends were here already. The older guy Tane hung out with—Evans—had come with his wife in the early evening and enjoyed the drink out on the back porch. The weather was perfect, the bar was crowded, and the drinks were selling out quickly.

"Where is he?" I asked when she returned, as if Marissa knew more than I did.

She frowned. "Dunno. But I bet Nina is going to be pissed if he doesn't show. What a cock-up," she said, clear disapproval in her voice.

Half an hour later, I stared at the last serving of the drink mix. Tane should have been here. This was his drink, but I didn't think he was coming. "Motherfucker," I mumbled under my breath and drained the bottle, serving the last of the special to a customer.

Hours later, when the crowd was starting to thin, my eyes caught on a familiar face at the end of the bar. Tane had arrived.

Even from a few steps away I could tell that he was drunk. His eyes were glassy and he was blinking too much.

I poured a glass of water and plunked it down in front of him. "Drink it," I snapped, but Tane just blinked.

I went off to take care of other customers. My shift would be over first and Marissa would work till closing, so I had only an hour or so left to go. When I next caught sight of Tane, he had a glass of beer in front of him, half empty. I stomped over.

"Where did you get that?"

He held up both hands. "Don't worry. I didn't—I didn't pour it myself," he said with half a smirk.

My eyes snapped to Marissa, who looked at me guiltily. *He's the boss*, she mouthed.

"Oi," Tane said, and I turned back to him. He squinted, pointing a thick finger at me. "You're in a bad mood."

I narrowed my eyes back. "You missed the cocktail special."

He groaned and closed his eyes. "That was tonight? I knew I was forgetting something." He swayed too far to the right and snapped his eyes open, regaining his balance. "Shh . . . don't tell Nina."

It was on the tip of my tongue to curse him out, but then his eyes started to droop and he swayed again. Even if I did curse him out, it wouldn't stick. I gave it a fifty-fifty chance that Tane wouldn't remember tomorrow.

Instead I caught Ron's eye over Tane's shoulder and snapped my fingers at him. "Ron!"

Ron looked up from where he was saying good night to a few departing customers and nodded at me. Lumbering to his feet, he stood next to Tane, hand on his shoulder, and said a few quiet words. I turned away and gritted my teeth.

I got back to work, and a few minutes later Ron returned from upstairs.

More customers left, and Marissa said she could handle the rest and suggested I leave.

Stepping out onto the back porch, I found Nina chatting with some of the locals. It was too dark out now to toss axes, but the summer evening was comfortable.

"Marissa says I'm good to leave if that's okay with you," I told her.

"Great," she said, standing up. "Let's go check you out."

We walked back inside together, Nina chatting excitedly about the drinks. "You'll have to do a bigger batch next week. We sold out so quickly. Oh!" She stopped us at the door to the office and glanced around. "What did Tane think?"

I tried to keep my voice respectful, mindful that this was complicated. "He didn't have one."

Nina's face flashed through emotions—surprise, concern, anger—and settled on disappointment. She looked back at me. "Is he here?"

"Ron took him upstairs," I said softly, and Nina nodded, tight-lipped.

I waited with sympathy while Nina tried to gather herself. She pinched the bridge of her nose. "Sorry. Sorry. It's just . . . I've been talking to some people about his drinking. He made the decision to quit playing, and I wonder all the time if he regrets it and that's why he drinks. Like . . . like he's avoiding the responsibility of making decisions again. I *want* him to be more involved. Instead he just . . . drinks. And it's getting worse."

I gently touched my palm to Nina's arm, giving her a squeeze of comfort. She put her hand over mine and blinked away tears. "Right," she said, shaking it off. "Let me get you your tips. After such a successful night, I don't need to drag you down with my troubles."

———

Having Sunday off meant that I stewed in my own anger the whole day while doing laundry and cleaning. I must have looked extra grumpy too, because hardly anyone in the hostel talked to me, and Iris was busy doing something or other with Chris.

"What did the laundry machine ever do to you?" said a voice with a thick French accent, startling me. I looked up to find one of my new hostel friends, Demi, smiling at me. "You're glaring at it like it insulted your mother."

I'd met Demi and her husband, Phillip, a few days ago. They were both French and gray-haired, traveling New Zealand in a rented van. We'd struck up a conversation when Demi had complimented my piercing, and then because she had a new septum piercing, we'd talked about the challenge of keeping it clean while traveling.

I raised an eyebrow. "Maybe it did insult my mother."

She chuckled. "You are off tomorrow, yes?"

I told her I was.

"Phillip and I are going to Somes Island for the day. Come join us. Our treat."

Somes Island was just a few miles from the city dock, an island in Wellington Harbour accessible only via a ferry. It had been on the list Nina had made for me, one of the places I could get to without a car. Demi, Phillip, and I boarded the ferry the next day, getting prime seats since it was a Monday, even though it was nearly peak tourist season.

"So what has you grouchy?" Phillip asked me after we had settled into our seats on the open-air top deck. Phillip was perhaps a decade or so older than Demi, and looked like a kind grandfather. A kind French grandfather. I liked him a lot.

I ranted for most of the twenty-five-minute trip, explaining the drink special to them, how Tane "forgot" about it, his general behavior around the bar, and Nina's disappointment. "The thing that really gets to me, though," I said, "was that it was, like, a *resigned* disappointment. Like this is Nina's lot in life, to have her brother be a constant problem."

Demi hummed as we disembarked the ferry onto Somes Island and got distracted making a plan of attack for the visit.

We walked the trails of the island, scoured the small pebbled beaches for seashells, and I even saw my first sheep, the cotton balls dotting the vibrant green landscape while they mowed the grass. We laughed as Phillip stepped into a sheep patty. And then we laughed doubly hard as he climbed over one of the stiles in the fields and got his jeans caught on the fence.

Demi and Phillip had packed a picnic lunch—cheese and bread and jam, very French—and we sat on one of the picnic tables overlooking the fields.

Demi told me about working with Greenpeace and some hair-raising stories of protests in the seventies. I felt like I'd had a sheltered life, and when I said this, Demi patted my cheek.

"You've just not lived yet," she said in her thick accent. And then she changed the subject. "You talked a lot about this Tane and how he lets his sister down. But he let you down too, no?"

"He let all the staff down."

"Ah, but you put in the most work. And you had gotten him to agree to the drink special and I am sure that he'll still be involved in making decisions."

"Yeah," I grumbled.

"It is tough that there is nothing you can do about it. Tane is his own man. He has to make his own path."

"That is not easy for some people," Phillip chimed in.

"But it's okay to be upset at him for yourself," Demi continued. She leaned over, pressing her shoulder into mine.

At the end of the day we boarded the ferry again. I'd walked miles and miles on Somes, and when I caught sight of myself in the mirror in the restroom, I did a double take. I was flushed from the exertion of the day, and I looked . . . relaxed. Talking with Demi and Phillip had helped me let go.

Well . . . I'd only been able to let *some* of my anger go. Just seeing Tane sitting at the bar when I arrived for my shift the next afternoon made my jaw clench. Of course he had a beer in front of him.

"Claire," Tane said, nodding at me as I clocked in.

"Hey." I kept my attention off Tane while Marissa clocked out and we moved the open tabs over to my name. She left and it was just me, Tane, and the customers out on the back deck with Ron. I pulled out some lemons to slice and restock, setting up as far down the bar as I could get from Tane.

"Ron says I may owe you an apology again."

I glanced down the bar to find Tane watching me, a little amusement on his face, and my anger came out of nowhere.

"What, that's funny? You find the whole thing amusing?" I said, incredulous.

The smirk dropped to a frown. "What, did I pour my own beer again?"

I stomped over and set my palms on the bar in front of him. Being upset with him might not change his behavior, but maybe it would be cathartic for me. "Everyone was disappointed you didn't come for the drink special." He opened his mouth, but I didn't let him talk. "Not just me—everyone: Marissa, Ron, *your sister.*

But I guess that's funny to you. Our fault, for expecting you to be involved."

My voice had risen, and when the door swung open behind Tane, I took a deep breath and stepped back, smiling at the couple walking in. "Hello! Are you here for the range or would you like a drink?"

I set them up in a corner booth and took their drink orders. When I returned from delivering the drinks, Tane had moved to the back of the bar, his usual spot, and I refused to look at him.

Group by group, customers came in and kept me busy. In the late afternoon, a few of Tane's normal crowd came in, ordered their drinks from me at the bar, and then joined Tane.

Later, when their table was littered with empty glasses, I forced myself to walk over with a tray to clean up.

"Another round?" I asked. It came out a little petulant.

Tane pushed back against the table, scowl in place. "How about one of the bottles of craft? Dealer's choice."

I looked around at the rest of the group and they all shook their heads.

Tane frowned at them. "What? It's still early."

"Sorry, mate," one of the guys said, "the missus wants me home early tonight."

"I've got to pick my teenager up from his study group," another said.

The last one stood up and clapped Tane on the back. "Don't worry, you'll have your fancy craft beer to keep you company, mate," and the others snickered.

When I returned with Tane's beer, the guys were gone and there was cash under their empty pint glasses.

For the next hour, Tane sat alone, nursing his beer.

I polished glasses and watched him out of the corner of my eye. He picked at the label while his eyes burned in a thousand-yard stare.

Decisively, he picked up the beer and took a swig, setting it back on the table with a soft clink, got up quietly, and, without fanfare, climbed the stairs to his apartment.

When I bused the table, the beer bottle was half full.

————

A week later I prepped the bar to open, setting out the menus and straightening the chairs. Light was streaming in from the big windows, the range out back a field of bright, vibrant green. I hummed along with the music playing overhead. I was in a good mood, having just been to the Te Papa Museum the day before. The museum was free and huge. I'd learned more about the history of New Zealand and the culture of the Māori people. I was beginning to feel less like I was escaping Boston and more like I was exploring New Zealand.

The door to Tane's apartment opened and the man himself stepped out.

I stopped humming and gave him a brittle smile. I hadn't seen him since that night I'd ripped into him. Come to think of it, it was kind of weird that Tane hadn't been around.

"Claire," he said, nodding at me. He wore a rugby jersey, bright red-and-blue-striped shorts, and black sneakers. "Is my sister around?"

"Out back."

"'Kay."

I kept my eyes down, wiping smudges from the glossy menus. After a moment, Tane stepped closer to the bar. I bit my lip, watching him scan the room and pick up a menu, as if he didn't know what was on it.

Did he want me to make him a drink? It was ten a.m. I didn't think I could really say no, but I also didn't *want* to.

I stepped around to the back of the bar and cleared my throat. "Can I get you something?"

Tane tossed the menu onto the bar and it spun in place. "What do you know about nonalcoholic beer?"

I raised an eyebrow. Tane had taken me by surprise. "Not much, to be honest. But it depends on the beer, I guess. I'd imagine you can get O'Doul's or whatnot from your supplier, but I bet there're also some local small-batch breweries doing non-alcs."

"Never heard of an O'Doul's before," Tane said.

We lapsed into silence and I kept my hands busy behind the bar, my mind spinning and a little flutter of hope in my chest.

"All right," he said. "I'll be back."

He didn't give me time to ask questions, just strode out the door. I wondered if he was serious about nonalcoholic beers? Maybe I would do some research in my off time tomorrow and see what non-alcs were available in Wellington. Most bars I'd worked at in Boston had at least one on the menu.

Fifteen minutes into our operating hours, I had just one group out back that Nina was instructing when Tane walked back through the doors. He lifted up a bag that clinked when he set it on the bar top, smiling victoriously.

"What's this?" I asked him.

"We're doing a tasting" was his response.

SEVEN

"What's even the point?"

Oddly, this question was not directed at the non-alcs in general, but at the particular one Tane had just tasted.

"Smells like nothing. Tastes like nothing," he said, swinging the bottle for another swig. The bottle looked comically small in his rugby ball–sized hands. "Won't get you drunk like nothing."

"That last one is the point," I said.

"Aye, that one I won't argue with, but come on. It should taste like something."

That was the fourth nonalcoholic beer we'd tasted, and sadly, it was the best one so far. Two had been abominations, one of them making me gag. We'd stopped opening a bottle each and split one instead. But most of the drink was going down the drain.

Tane pulled the paper bag closer. The cool bottles had left condensation behind and the bag was tearing down the side.

"There're three more left," he said after counting.

I stuck out my tongue. "I need, like . . . a cracker."

Tane slipped off his barstool and strode back into the kitchen, returning a few minutes later with some cheese and crackers.

I popped one into my mouth and Tane did the same. He chewed and swallowed quickly before setting his jaw.

"I did want to say that I was sorry," Tane said, meeting my eye, and I choked on my cracker for a second.

"For missing the drink special," he continued when I caught my breath, my cheeks flushing. "I know you worked hard on it. And I should have been there because it does matter."

"Oh. Thanks," I said, eyebrows raised in surprise.

"I apologized to everyone else, too: Nina, Marissa, Ron . . ." He gave me a small smile. "Anyway, let's try another one, eh?" He reached into the bag for the next beer.

The apology was more than I'd been expecting, so I let it go and placed a new glass on the bar. Tane cracked open the next bottle, pouring half into the glass and saving the bottle for himself.

We locked eyes from across the bar.

"It's Bavarian." Tane sounded doubtful.

"We've been fooled before," I said solemnly.

After a moment's hesitation, I raised my glass. Tane clinked his beer against mine, and we took a small whiff of the aroma.

He raised an eyebrow. "It smells like beer. . . ."

"It's definitely light." I took a bigger sniff. I looked into my glass, hesitating. "All right . . . I'm going in."

We sipped at the same time. Tane's brow furrowed as he rolled the beer around on his tongue. Since it was still in our mouths, that was a good sign.

It was light and weak, not a great beer but . . .

"Not bad," Tane said.

"It tastes like a PBR."

"What's a PBR?"

"It's a . . . well, just a cheap redneck beer."

"Yeah, okay, redneck as." The corner of Tane's mouth twitched up as he took another sip. "This is the winner so far. Two more to go."

Instead of pouring this one down the drain, I set them both to the side as Tane opened the next one. I finally had to ask: "Why are we trying nonalcoholic beers?"

Tane glanced at me and then toward the back of the bar, where Nina was outside demonstrating. I held out my glass at a tilt and Tane poured the rich brown liquid in. He hesitated, vulnerability flashing over his face before his features hardened. "One of my mates said something the other day. And I realized I'd become the butt of a joke. The washed-up loser whose sister has to take care of him."

"You need better friends. This was those schmucks you drink with all the time?" Anger sharpened my tone and Tane smirked in amusement.

"Nah, one of my friends from the game. The guys around here are all right, you know. But they've got lives. Kids. Wives. I need to change." He nodded at the glass. "I think it starts with this. Giving up the drink."

"I think that sounds great," I said softly. "And this"—I gestured to the empty bottles—"will keep you hanging out with your friends. Will you be able to get these from a distributor?"

"Maybe. I'm not sure; Nina handles all of that. But at least we will have a basic foundation, right? We will know how bad it can be."

We clinked drinks again and brought the rims to our noses. Immediately my eyes watered as a foul, stale smell hit me.

"What the fuck?" Tane shouted. The smell was so bad, he stood up from the bar, holding the offensive bottle aloft as far as possible. I choked on the smell and dumped my glass down the drain as quickly as I could. "How is this shit legal?" Tane asked.

The door to the deck opened and Nina walked in. Her face flipped like a switch from laughing with the customers to seeing me and Tane, empty bottles surrounding us and pint glasses full of amber liquid. All traces of humor disappeared.

"Tane . . ." she said, low and disappointed.

"Oi, don't fuss," Tane said, gentling his voice. "It's non-alc."

The switch flipped again, and Nina's face lit up.

"Here, you wanna try one?" Tane offered the half-full bottle to Nina and I bit down on a laugh.

"Oh, I'm so proud of you." Nina took the drink from his hands and pinched his cheek. "How've they been so far? I bet . . ." She tried to take a sip and choked, not expecting the foulness.

Tane bent over laughing as Nina gagged and slammed the bottle down on the bar, sloshing beer—in name only—over the surface. She shoved Tane out of the way, reaching for a handful of cheese and crackers from the plate.

She shoveled them in, chewing furiously and giving her brother the stink eye. He was still laughing, even as Nina started to pelt him with crackers. Tane ducked a few and then started catching them, swatting them out of the air and into his mouth.

Nina eventually ran out of ammo. "That was just grotty," she said, sticking her tongue out as if trying to get rid of the flavor. "Ugh, I can taste it in my tonsils."

"We've still got one more," I said, wriggling my eyebrows at her.

"Fuck no. Sorry, bro, I love you, but not enough to drink that. 'Sides, I need some drinks for the couple outside."

Tane cleaned up crackers while I shook a cocktail and Nina pulled from the kegs. She carried the drinks off, and I came back to stand opposite Tane, who'd removed our final non-alc from the tattered bag.

He twisted the cap off with his bare hand and picked up my glass. Tane watched the pour, tilting the glass like a pro to avoid the head. He didn't meet my eye, but he was still flushed from the laughter over pranking his sister.

"Here's to the last one," I said.

His eyes flickered over my face, but he said nothing as we clinked glasses and sniffed and tasted the last beer.

He waffled his hand. "'S all right."

I nodded. "Not as good as the Bavarian, not as bad as the rest."

"A middling beer." He reached across the bar and tasted the Bavarian again. "Makes this one taste better, eh."

The front door opened and customers entered. I excused myself from Tane and took care of them, settling them in a booth with drink menus.

When I came back, Tane was behind the bar, washing glasses and draining bottles.

"I can take care of that," I said. "It is my job."

"Nah, she'll be right."

The door opened again, and the slow trickle of guests for the day began. To my surprise, Tane stayed back behind the bar. When he didn't have anything to do, he cocked a hip on the cooler and sipped his non-alc.

Sometimes our eyes locked, and I had to shake it off and remind myself to look away. Having Tane behind the bar with me made his presence more real. Instead of snatches of laughter from the back, he was right here with me, and I'd hear bits of conversation or the tail end of a joke he'd make with a customer as I'd catch sight of him.

Even his laughter felt different to me. More like pure Tane, even if I had no idea how I knew what that would sound like.

But he was there, all afternoon and till the end of my shift.

Sober.

————

After the success of the gin fizz, Nina had encouraged me to come up with some more suggestions and we had scheduled a tasting for seventeen days from the night of the drink special, a Tuesday. I was pretty pleased with myself.

My bank account balance was low, but Nina gave me some cash in advance when I told her my ideas. On a Sunday morning, I woke up way earlier than normal and walked from my hostel to the farmers market.

The supermarkets had produce I had never seen before, or at least varieties of things that were familiar but different. Golden kiwis, with bright yellow flesh instead of green, and huge golden mangoes—everything here was golden, apparently.

But the farmers market brought on even more treats. I used my own money to splurge on stroopwafels and Chinese jianbing pancakes, wolfing them down as I huddled against the wind. But I was also after anything I could use in a cocktail. Fruits and herbs went into my bag. I had no clue what many of them were, but I wrote down what the market vendors told me and bookmarked things for later.

Now I had three of the staff sitting in front of me, Nina and two of the other bartenders, Marissa and Alec. Tane sat a few seats down, eating breakfast he'd picked up from the takeaway place around the corner and fiddling with his phone.

"We've got four new drinks to try out," I said, gesturing to the chilled glasses in front of me. "I'll pour you a bit of each, but don't finish it if you don't want to. Some of us have to work, unfortunately." Myself included.

I grabbed the first chilled shaker from the cooler and added ice to the premixed drink. "This first one is a feijoa margarita." I'd found the small green fruits in the frozen foods section of the grocery store—they were out of season now— and I'd added the puree to the classic margarita recipe. The flavor was unlike anything I'd ever tasted before—a little sweet, a little citrusy. Perfect to go with tequila.

"This is a good idea. People get sick of feijoas in the winter," Alec commented.

I mixed the next drink up while my taste-testers chatted and sipped. We sampled a kiwi cooler with slices of golden kiwis floating in the glass and a manuka honey lemon martini.

"And this one," I said, pulling out five clean highball glasses and dividing the shaker contents between them, "has Tane's name on it." I slid the fifth glass down the bar.

He looked up at his name, and his eyebrows drew together as he took in the cocktail. "I'm not going to taste it, Claire."

I struggled to tamp down a grin and I tipped my chin up at the drink. "It's a non-alc gin. I call it a Golden Non-Rickey." Thick cubes of golden mango floated in the liquid. It was my favorite of the drinks, primarily because of the mango. The juices had overflowed as I'd diced and peeled, dripping down my forearms. It was nothing like any mango I'd ever tasted before, big and golden and juicy. An entire mango had disappeared into my mouth before I'd even made the first cocktail.

Tane was still staring at the drink.

"Look," I said, "I know you're probably more of a beer guy, but you liked the gin fizz I made and

I thought it would be fun for you to try something else. I can make you a regular ole G and T if you want with this fake gin. And"—I turned, looking at Nina—"I can make it a real Golden Rickey if you'd prefer."

I had made the nonalcoholic version for everyone else, too, and they sipped the drink attentively.

"Huh," Alec said. "I don't think I could tell it's nonalcoholic in a taste test."

We talked about the gin and I pulled up the website on my phone and brought out the bottle. My eyes kept finding Tane's in excitement. I wanted to watch him drink it. I wanted to see his surprise, or even . . . pleasure at enjoying this drink. I knew he didn't normally do mixed drinks, but after the nonalcoholic beers were such a letdown, I wanted to give Tane a better choice.

After all, he was doing the hard work. I was kind of . . . proud? It felt weird, especially after how we'd first met, but I wanted Tane to succeed, even more so when I saw how happy it made Nina.

But maybe a cocktail just wasn't enough.

He stirred with the cardboard straw, sniffed, and took an experimental sip. His face didn't show much reaction, but he went in for a second sip before Nina distracted me with more questions.

When I looked up again, Tane was gone, and my stomach sank. The glass sat empty on the bar. What did that mean? Did he enjoy it, or was he upset about it? No one else seemed to notice that he'd left.

Tasting officially over, Marissa and Alec got behind the bar with me and Alec lined up a row of shot glasses.

"What are you doing?" Nina asked.

"Tasting it straight. And we can't get drunk," Alec explained.

"Shots! Shots! Shots!" Marissa whooped while Nina just shook her head at our antics and went back to the office.

When the novelty of the faux-gin wore off—one shot for me, three for Alec—Marissa and Alec went home and I was back to my regular workday, albeit a quiet one.

Nina was in and out, asking me questions about ingredients and pricings, and I could tell that she was excited about making a change. My heart warmed to see her giddy, but I wondered where her brother was.

"Hey, what about Tane?" I asked her after we discussed placing an order for flavored simple syrup.

"What about him?" she said, distracted.

I shrugged, not wanting Nina to know how much it had bothered me that Tane had disappeared. "Where is he?"

At that, Nina looked up and glanced around. A crease formed between her eyebrows and she gave me a long look.

"Why are you so concerned, Claire?" she asked, and her eyebrows went from anxious to wiggling.

I scoffed and rolled my eyes, feeling my face heat up. It was *not* that. "I'm not into your brother. I made him a drink; the least he could do was give me some feedback."

"I didn't say anything about you being into him," Nina said, a slow smile creeping over her face. "He drank the whole thing. And I bet you twenty dollars he comes back around before the end of your shift."

"Oh, come on, that's a shoo-in bet. He's down here most nights."

Nina smirked over her shoulder at me while walking back to her office. "Most nights *you're* here."

My face flushed further and she cackled, slamming the door on her laughter.

Three hours later I was thinking I should have taken Nina up on that bet. Tane hadn't come down and we were starting to close up. Two servers had been sent home already, the kitchen staff was gone, and I was restocking for the next day.

I heard a door opening and turned, expecting Nina to be coming in from outside, but instead Tane stood opposite me at the bar. I froze, a bottle of tequila under one arm and a handful of limes in the other. "Oh! Tane. Hi."

"Hey," he said, shifting stools around to lean onto the bar. His mouth was turned down, eyes serious and steady.

I was tempted to make a joke about tequila shots, but that wasn't appropriate with Tane being sober. Instead I just put the tequila and limes down and leaned on the bar, mirroring him, my forearms just a few inches away from his. "Are you okay?" I asked quietly.

Tane broke eye contact and looked down at his laced fingers. Nerves fluttered in my stomach as I looked at his face. This close I could see little crow's-feet around his eyes and a scar on one earlobe.

Tane took a deep breath and I turned my attention away from his ear—why was I staring at it anyway?—to his eyes.

"I just wanted to say thank you for all the effort you put in today. With the gin, and the cocktails. But mostly the gin. That was . . . nice."

He looked at me then, so open and genuine and trusting. The flutter moved from my stomach up to my chest and I smiled. Tane turned his face away again with a flash of his white teeth. "I also have a sober coach. And one of the things we talk about is finding people who support us. And I think it's lucky that even though I own a bar, I've found that kind of support here. With you. And Nina, of course."

I pressed my lips together. Tane wouldn't understand, but I was feeling the same way about this place. Tane and Nina, my other friends at the bar and the hostel, they didn't realize how they were supporting me, but it had been a long time since I'd worried about Devon. That was the gift Tane and Nina had given me.

As if summoned, a door opened and Nina's voice filtered in over the music. "Tane, what are you doing here?" Nina pressed an exaggerated hand on her hip. "I thought for *sure* you were in for the night."

She looked too damn smug for her own good, but the interruption made me realize how close Tane and I were to each other. He moved first, straightening and throwing a perplexed look at Nina. "Am I not allowed to be down here?"

Nina's face turned innocent. "Nah, you're fine, bro. I'm going to go outside and clean up the deck. You hanging out?"

"Yeah." Tane looked at me. "Can you make me a drink?"

I mixed Tane a mocktail, and he sat across from me while I kept working on inventory. We talked a little bit about the drinks and then he asked how my new hostel was going before the topic shifted. "You know something else I'm doing?" he asked.

"What?"

"I started coaching," he said, grinning.

"Coaching rugby?" I paused, half in the reach-in cooler, and Tane nodded.

"That's awesome," I said, pulling my attention back to the task.

"There's actually a game next Monday night. I think Nina and a few other staff are coming. You should come too."

"Yeah, that sounds fun."

"Good," Tane said, standing. "I'll clear out. So you can finish cleaning up and go home." He shoved his hands into his pockets, shuffling a little on his feet. "Good night, Claire. Thanks again."

———

"Claire, what are you doing here?" Marissa looked at me, confused, and checked the time on her phone. "Your shift doesn't start for another hour."

"Nina asked me to come in early, since we've got a bachelorette party for twenty today."

She shook her head. "That's tomorrow."

"Is it?" I pulled out my phone, thumbing through text messages until I found the right one. *Damn it.* "Fuck, she did say Friday. Son of a bitch."

Marissa tilted her head toward the backyard. "It's a nice day—go relax in the back." She spun around, searching the shelves until she found what she was looking for. "You wanna drink?" she asked, wiggling the bottle of fake gin at me.

"Nah, that's okay. I'll play games on my phone or something. Thanks, though."

I pushed open the back door and found that I wasn't the only person who'd had this idea. There was a group of four people over on one of the targets, and Tane was on the porch, stretched out and keeping an eye on them. It was lovely out, a sunny and warm New Zealand summer day.

"Claire?" he said, surprise in his voice.

I shrugged, chagrined. "Came in for work too early."

He shifted his weight, sitting up and pulling his legs in a bit more. "Want a seat? Or . . . do you want to play?" His chin tilted up, drawing my attention to the rows of targets that lined the lawn.

I cocked an eyebrow at him. "I've never thrown an axe before."

Tane heaved himself up, and I followed him as he made his way down to the range. He picked a lane, with space between us and the guests, but not so far that he couldn't keep an eye on them.

Each lane had a U-shaped bench with a low table in the center that stored scorecards. The trellises of grapes served as dividers between the lanes, and the targets themselves were large wooden boxes, the open end facing the seats, the bottoms of the boxes painted with a red-and-white target.

Tane pulled an axe out of a small box nailed to the post. "First rule: Don't walk away with the axe. The weapons never leave this area between the post and the target, okay? Don't take them back to the seats, and don't hand them to someone. You throw, retrieve, and put it back into the box, okay?"

I brought my brows low, mimicking the seriousness in Tane's face. "Okay."

He showed me how to throw, putting his grip on the handle—the haft—just right, raising the axe overhead and then chucking it at the target.

With a solid *thwack* it sank into the wood.

"How do you get it to rotate right?"

"Practice" was his answer. "You'll start to get a feel for the way the axe rotates." He demonstrated again, and after retrieving the axe, he put it in the box. "Your turn."

I grabbed the haft, pulling the axe out of the box. I replicated the grip, and pulled it back over my head. Using my arms, I tried to chuck the axe at the target. Instead it buried into the grass a few feet short of the target.

"Wow," I said, shaking out my shoulders. "That's heavy."

"We have smaller ones," he offered.

I shook my head. "Let me try again." I retrieved the axe and gave it another go, this time releasing way earlier than I had before. It spun and hit the top right of the target, bouncing off and hitting the ground.

"Close," Tane encouraged me.

I tried again and again, finally figuring out how it felt to release the axe with the right rotation to get it to land blade-first. After a few successful throws, I put the axe into the box. "How do you keep score?"

Tane showed me the scorecard, and told me how you could score several variations of the game, like darts. I wrote my name at the top, and then Tane's.

"Okay, sir, let's see how good you are."

He rubbed his hands together. "Prepare to be annihilated."

This time there was no messing around. Tane strode up, grabbed the axe from the box, and then threw it one-handed, easily sinking it into the bull's-eye.

"One-handed. Is that regulation play?" I teased.

Tane smacked his bicep with his palm. "Playing with a handicap."

I snorted, and took my next shot. Tane schooled me, as expected, but toward the end of the game, my arms were getting weak. Even trying with all my might, I couldn't quite get the axe up toward the circles in the upper corners.

But then, after one of his throws, Tane tripped a little bit returning to the bench.

I reached out, but then hesitated a moment, remembering that he'd retired because he'd injured his ACL multiple times. And Tane had already been defensive about it, so I needed to be gentle. "Are you okay?"

He eased down next to me but didn't meet my eye. "Yeah. Sometimes my knee gets a little wobbly." He rubbed his right knee absentmindedly and I thought about that first night we met when he toppled over—very drunk —but maybe his knee had exacerbated the situation.

"Do you think it's less wobbly now that you are sober?"

He gave it some thought. "Maybe. But it also aches more."

"I bet it does." Of course it didn't surprise me that the drinking was self-medicating.

"Every retired athlete has pains from old wounds. My da couldn't get out of bed sometimes. Slipped discs."

I thought back to my conversation with Nina and my cyber stalking. "He's a retired rugby player too, right?"

Tane nodded. "Was. Papa's been gone for ten years." Before I could apologize for my misstep, he went on. "He was the reason I played, and the reason I retired. I could have had another surgery, more PT, but I knew it was only a matter of time. Someday a hit would take me down and it wouldn't be my decision anymore. But it doesn't mean I don't regret it." His face was pinched. "Would I have had another year? Or three?"

"That couldn't have been easy," I said softly.

He let out a dark chuckle. "I thought about my mum and how much of a burden my da had been on her. She'd practically raised us herself, Papa always off at games. And then when he couldn't play anymore, she took care of him." Tane's eyes were unfocused, his memories all he could see. "I didn't want that to happen. You know, I've got no wife, my mum's aging, Nina's got her family. But somehow I became the burden anyway, the drunk who couldn't keep his shit together." Tane's eyes fell on his hands, clasped between his knees. His focus sharpened and he picked at a cuticle. "What about your parents?"

I sighed. "They live in Boston. I haven't talked to them since I arrived here. I'm not even sure they know where I am." Tane frowned, but waited for me to continue. "They were always a little distant. They had me and my sister close together—Irish twins—and I think it was more than they wanted to handle. And then, a couple years ago, I needed help and they didn't really care." I shrugged, thinking once again how thankful I was to have Iris. "I think they didn't like the responsibility."

Tane hummed. "I can understand that. If you start to doubt your decisions, it's easier to just not make any. Not that it's the right thing to do," he added quickly. "But that's like what I did with alcohol, you know? Used it as an excuse to have a good time instead of being responsible."

I nudged Tane's shoulder with mine. He barely moved. "You're doing good now. You decided to give me a chance with my drinks." I put a hint of a tease into my voice, trying to leaven the conversation and leave Tane with something other than disappointment in himself.

It worked, and he chuckled, this time a little lighter. "Pretty pleased with that, aren't you?"

We smiled at each other, holding eye contact for a bit longer than we normally would have. "Anyway," I said, checking my watch and breaking the moment. "I've still got another half an hour before my shift, but I don't think I'm going to have the energy for round two. I do have to be able to reach the top shelf tonight."

Tane accepted the change of topic, dusting his hands off. "Hold on, I've got an alternative."

He strode over and rummaged around a cabinet set against the wall of the porch, and emerged with six shiny metal discs. "Throwing stars," he said when he returned to the seats, handing me three.

"What? No way! That's awesome. How do you throw them?"

Tane demonstrated, and they were easier to throw than I'd thought they'd be. I held them between two fingers over my shoulder and flicked them at the target.

He took the row next to me, and we launched the throwing stars at the targets until Marissa came out to find me and call me in for my shift.

"Thanks, Tane," I said, setting the discs down on the table. "That was fun."

"You're a proper employee now," he teased.

"Because I know how to throw an axe?"

"Yeah," he said with a laugh. "But maybe stick with the throwing stars."

EIGHT

I'd spent the weekend making sure Tane and Nina were aware that I knew absolutely nothing about rugby. Nina insisted I come to the youth game anyway, and offered to pick me up.

I was out front of the hostel at five on Monday. Nina drove a beater, an old station wagon with the Toyota logo on the hood, but a model I didn't recognize.

I was, however, surprised to find only one seat available: the front passenger seat was occupied by Nina's husband, Hemi, a heavyset guy with glasses who seemed close to Nina's age and with similar dark skin. In the back were their two daughters in car seats. For some reason I hadn't thought about Nina's family joining us.

"Oh, hi," I said to no one in particular.

"Claire, you remember Hemi?"

Hemi waved from his seat.

"Yeah, hey, Hemi."

"Girls, say hi to Claire. Sorry, you'll have to squeeze in between them."

I opened the back door and ducked down, contorting myself to fit in between the front seat and one of the girls, who helpfully kicked me in the boob.

Once plopped down in the middle seat, I gave Nina wide eyes through the rearview mirror. I was not adept at kids. Usually when Nina or Hemi brought them into the bar, we kept a fair distance between us while I worked and they played.

"Oh, relax, Claire. They don't bite."

Nope, just kick.

"Which is which again?" I asked. Okay, Natty, on my left, was older, maybe three or four. Old enough to kick me in the boob and giggle at me. Nora, her younger sister, on my right, gurgled and stuck her hand in her mouth. "Are you excited to watch some rugby?"

Natty giggled. "You talk funny."

"Who me?" I laid it on thick. "I'm just sitting here with your sistah in the cah."

The girls both giggled now and I relaxed a little on the drive to the field. This was my first time to see most of the staff outside of work, outside of my uniform. It was a little chilly, so I'd dressed in jeans and a long-sleeve shirt with a retro logo that read "Live and Let Die" with a D20 over one of my boobs.

Nina had brought folding chairs, so we hauled them out of the trunk and across the grassy fields to the crowd. Young boys, preteens, were running warm-ups on the field, looking like any high school sports team getting ready for a game. Tane was easy to spot, pacing on the sidelines and shouting at the boys. He was dressed in a bright blue jersey with matching rugby shorts—short shorts—with a flash of gray Lycra peeking out from underneath.

There were a few familiar faces there already, and others who I assumed were parents. Hemi and the girls wandered off to play with some kids closer to the girls' ages. I settled in and greeted the staff members around us. Nina opened a cooler between our chairs and I picked out a beer.

"Everyone's pretty excited, and I'm a bit surprised Tane even invited us to come," she said.

"Why is that?"

She sipped her beer. "It's the first time I think I've seen him interested in rugby again since his injury."

"That's a lot of change since I met him."

"It is," Nina agreed. "Almost gives me hope."

A whistle blew and practice drills turned into what I was sure must have been a game. Nina tried to explain the ins and outs of rugby to me. I'd thought that maybe since I didn't have much knowledge about football, soccer, or rugby, I wouldn't have to reconfigure a sports thing I already knew and would have an easier time following . . . but that didn't appear to be the case. It got complicated. There was union rugby, rugby sevens, and touch rugby. The game being played was touch rugby in a summer coaching clinic.

But the weather was nice, the company was chatty, and I had a few beers. It was fun to watch Tane stalk up and down the sidelines and talk to the kids. The kids were in the ten-to-twelve range, I thought, and Tane often bent over, hands on his knees, to get down to their level.

Sometimes he bent over facing away from me. He might have gone a little soft in his retirement, but he still had quite the bubble butt.

I wondered about his knee, and how it was doing with all the pacing and bending, but I was sure Tane would have been affronted at the idea that he couldn't do something like coaching a youth league. It didn't seem to bother him, though.

After two forty-minute halves, the game was called, and Tane's boys won. We cheered as the teams shook hands and Tane's team celebrated. Nina and I stood off to the side, watching Tane as kids bounced around him. Some of them were the boys from the team, but some were younger, little siblings of the team members.

"Line-outs! Line-outs!" became the chant.

Tane groaned. "All right, all right, ease up and line up."

The kids cheered and followed directions, getting in an orderly line facing Tane. Another coach twirled a rugby ball in his hands, just to the side of the end of the line. The first kid, a redhead wearing the jersey of the losing team, at Tane's signal, turned around and backed away from the line. Tane stood to the side and counted off—three, two, one—before stepping in behind the kid and grabbing his shorts, lifting the boy up overhead. The coach snapped the ball up and the kid caught it, practically squealing in delight.

I winced, thinking that would lead to one hell of a wedgie.

Tane let the kid down, and the kid tossed the ball back to the coach and ran to the end of the line.

"Oi, one each, scamp. Nice try." Tane pointed off to the sidelines and the kid slumped his shoulders dramatically before trotting over to his family.

"What is this?" I whispered to Nina.

"They're called line-outs. They don't do 'em much in the younger grades, but it's good practice for them to learn."

We watched as Tane hefted a young girl, maybe eight years old, over his head and let her legs dangle down as she caught a gentle toss from the coach. He didn't let her down, though, bracing his arms and letting her squirm up in the air.

"He's going to tire himself out," Nina remarked. "Silly man." We took our seats again, content to watch.

But Tane made it through the whole line of kids, three dozen or so, most of them younger. By the end he was sweaty, wiping his forehead as he walked toward me and his sister.

The evening was still bright, a long, late January day making the stadium lights unnecessary. Tane accepted a bottle of water from Nina and chugged it down.

"I don't remember being that heavy at that age."

"You weren't. You were heavier," Nina teased.

Tane let himself fall back onto the grass. The loose edge of his shorts rode up a bit and I diverted my eyes, feeling very puritan. All that muscle. All that thigh. Yowzah.

Natty and Nora ran up, the older one pumping her arms and legs while the younger one toddled behind—I couldn't remember which was which anymore—and piled onto their uncle. It reminded me of a video I once saw of a sugar glider trying to play with a Saint Bernard. They bounced around and were mostly ignored, content to play a version of King of the Mountain while Tane greeted Hemi.

Until one of them accidentally landed on Tane's junk. Then Hemi wisely took the girls back to the playground.

"So, Claire," Nina said, leaning back and pulling me into the conversation. "What did you think of your first rugby game?"

Tane's eyes snapped to mine and he smirked. "A rugby virgin, eh?"

"I don't know if watching a youth league game really popped my cherry," I joked.

Nina and Tane threw their heads back in laughter. "Too true," Nina chuckled. A wail came up from the playground and we looked over to see Hemi picking the older girl up off the ground. Hemi glanced over at us.

"Well, that's my signal," Nina said, getting up from the chair. "I'll be back."

Tane broke the silence between us. "I know rugby's not that popular in the States. Which sports do you watch?"

"Honestly, not many. Growing up in Boston, you pretty much have to be a Red Sox fan, but I was never into the sportings."

Tane ignored my use of *sportings.* "What do the Red Sox play?"

"Baseball," I said. "I don't think we have many sports in common with New Zealand on a professional level, except maybe soccer."

He scoffed, either at the word *soccer*—football here—or just American sports in general.

I wanted to know more, but I wasn't sure how much Tane would be willing to talk, since he'd shut down our last conversation about rugby. But things had changed, so maybe I wouldn't put my foot in my mouth this time. "Which city did you play for?"

He told me, and explained that that was the regular season. "But then there's the national team, and, by the way, the States have one and they're terrible. We play around the world against other countries. The Rugby World Cup is every four years. The New Zealand team is without a doubt the best rugby team in the world—rugby union, anyways." He grumbled something about Fijians and sevens that I didn't understand.

"Who's the second best? Or, like, your biggest rival?"

Tane leaned back on his hands. "South Africa. During apartheid, when the New Zealand team toured, some Māori and Pacific Islanders players were purposefully left out of the tour because their government didn't allow mixed-race teams."

"Oh my God," I said, aghast.

Tane lifted an eyebrow. "There's more to sports than just the game," he teased. "But it's better now that apartheid is gone. It's a friendlier rivalry now."

"I couldn't imagine bringing racial tension onto the field too. Rugby already sounds pretty rough."

"It is," he agreed.

"How is your leg? You said before that it still hurts."

He shrugged. "It's all right." He looked down and rubbed his knee, and I noticed a faint scar over his kneecap.

"Would you be able to play at all? Even just a fun game?"

Tane frowned before opening and closing his mouth. Finally he said, in a sad and distant voice, "I'm not sure I would want to."

"Well," Nina interrupted us, "Nora's getting cranky, so it's time to head home. Ready, Claire?"

"I can take her back," Tane said, rising to his feet.

"You sure, bro?" Nina said, relief in her voice. "That would be great. You don't mind, right, Claire?"

I shook my head, and Tane and I helped Nina pack up the chairs while Hemi strapped the girls into the car.

"See you tomorrow," Nina said, before reaching up to bring Tane's face down to her level. "So proud of you. You make a great coach."

"Yeah, thanks," Tane said, kissing her cheek.

Nina drove off and I followed Tane to a black truck in the near-empty parking lot.

Tane started the engine up while I crawled into the passenger seat. It was a big vehicle, befitting a guy his size.

"Did Nina tell you," he said as he pulled out of the lot, "that we picked a nonalcoholic beer from the distributor?"

"Yeah?" I said, perking up. "That's exciting."

"They only carry a few choices for beers, so I picked the Bavarian. It would be nice to have variety, but I think I'll be the only one drinking them."

"You never know," I said. "What about the gin?"

Tane's face scrunched up. "Yeah, nah. That's harder to do. I'm working directly with the company myself."

The company I'd gotten the gin from had other options too, and Tane and I debated which one would be best to stock the bar with.

"If no one's going to drink it besides me, then I should just order whatever I want."

"But margaritas are the most popular cocktail. So if you want someone to randomly come up and order a non-alc," I argued, "you should go with tequila. Plus, you can flavor it easily. There are tons of choices with tequila."

"I don't like tequila" was Tane's response.

"Well, what is your favorite, then? I've never seen you order a cocktail."

"Gin and tonic."

I flopped over onto the window and pretended to snore. "BOR-ring!"

"What's your favorite?"

"Any kind of fizz, really. I love the texture of the shaken egg whites."

"Egg whites?" Tane said, staring at me as we pulled up to a light. "There are egg whites in it?"

"You drank one," I pointed out.

"I did?"

"The gin fizz I made! With the candied orange? How did you not know this?"

"I drink beers," he defended.

"You own a bar."

"Fine, point made. I don't pay enough attention," he grumbled, sulking.

"Don't athletes love eggs? Protein and all that? Rocky Balboa slurping down a glass of raw eggs?"

Tane stuck his tongue out in disgust. "That's old-school. Now we have protein shakes and supplements instead. Less salmonella."

"Stop it," I said, swatting his shoulder. "You didn't get sick."

"I know, I know," he conceded. "I trust you."

That made me feel warm all over. "Thank you."

"You're welcome." Tane tapped the steering wheel with a finger as a comfortable silence settled over us for a moment. "Why don't we order a non-alc tequila to test out, eh?"

"Deal."

NINE

"Tane needs to bring a girlfriend to our cousin's wedding next weekend," Nina said out of the blue.

There were seven of us in the dining area, working to get ready to open on a Saturday. A few servers were polishing silverware, one was rolling the forks and knives into black napkins, and I was restocking purees.

Most noticeable was Tane, who sat at the bar, going through some paperwork. His head snapped up and he stared at Nina through the mirrors behind the bar. When she didn't look up from wiping down menus, he spun around in his seat.

"I don't need a girlfriend."

"Our cousin's getting married in a week in Auckland, and it's kind of a big deal. Tane's got a plus-one and he really needs to bring a girlfriend."

"I do not need a girlfriend," he insisted.

"See, he recently told our mother that he's been seeing someone to stop her from setting him up. And I know he doesn't want to admit to lying to her."

We all glanced at Tane, who flushed. "She keeps trying to set me up with Shivani's awful niece."

"And the few times he's brought 'dates' to family events, it has not gone over well. So he can't bring just anyone."

Tane emitted a growl. "I'm not interested in a fake girlfriend. No one does that in real life."

"My brother, who *once hired an escort to attend an awards ceremony with him*," Nina said, still not looking at him, "could absolutely use a fake date for this wedding."

"That was one time! And stop talking about me as if I'm not here."

"I think Claire should go," Maureen, one of the servers, said, glancing up from the silverware.

"Wait, what?" Tane and I said together.

Nina gestured with her rag. "Claire, you don't put up with Tane's shit. And it'll be fun. Aside from her burning desire to see Tane settled down, Mum's really charming."

"No. No, no, no." While the words came out of my mouth, Tane's eyes narrowed at me from the other side of the bar. "Why can't he just break up with his made-up girlfriend?"

"I'm right here!" Tane's voice was rising.

Nina turned in her chair, finally addressing Tane directly. "Do you want to break up with your fake girlfriend? Shivani's niece lives in Auckland —I wouldn't be surprised if you show up without a date and suddenly Kalini is invited to the post-wedding brunch at Mum's."

Tane's face turned sullen. "No," he sulked.

Nina grinned and went back to ignoring her brother. "Claire, you can pretend to be Tane's fake girlfriend for the weekend. It'll be fun."

I looked at her skeptically. "Don't you need me here at the bar?"

"Right, she has to—" Tane tried to cut in.

Nina talked right over him. "I already checked with Tamati. He'll cover the bar."

"I'm not an escort," I huffed at her.

"I'll make sure you get your own room," she said.

"What?" I squeaked, horrified. "Sharing a room was on the table? Nina, no."

"Come on, it would be fun. You'd get to see Auckland for a few days while Tane's busy with family stuff."

"Don't I get a say in any of this?" Tane's voice was weary, already giving up the battle.

"How about I sweeten the pot, Claire? You and Tane would be driving up the day before the wedding—"

"Wait, *driving up*? You want me in the car with Tane for how long? Why can't we fly?"

"Eight hours," Nina said cheerfully.

Out of the corner of my eye, I saw Tane gesture at his body. "Does not fit in commercial aircraft," he said, and winced, "comfortably."

"—but on the way back, you can take an extra day and stop anywhere you want."

Ooooohhh. Nina had gotten my attention and she knew it.

"Absolutely not." Tane ran a hand down his face. "I'm not going to do that tourist shit."

"One day stopping with your own private tour guide." Nina held her hands up, Vanna Whiting at Tane. "He comes complete with a scowl."

I pursed my lips in thought.

"Hobbiton?" she said.

My ears perked up and my heart practically skipped a beat. "I'm listening."

"Hotel room there and two tickets to the Evening Banquet," Nina negotiated.

I hesitated and bit my lip. Hobbiton was out in the middle of nowhere, so I'd have to take the bus to visit it by myself. And the Evening Banquet was expensive.

"Claire." Tane turned to me. "You'll be stuck spending the whole weekend with me. I'm grouchy. You don't like me."

My eyes flickered between Tane and Nina. She gave me these big, hopeful eyes. And I thought about how excited she was over Tane's sobriety and I knew this was really important to her. She may not want to say it and embarrass Tane, or show a lack of faith in him, but I bet she was hoping I would be some kind of moral support or buffer for him.

"Fine," I said, and she whooped. "But when we get there, you have to stay close, because I don't know anyone. And Hobbiton better be really good."

"Deal."

We shook hands while Tane sighed, exasperated. I may have sold my soul for the Lord of the Rings fandom, but I didn't care. A weekend in Auckland and a night in Hobbiton would more than make up for it.

"Thanks for coming. Have a good night!" I called out to our last customers. Being that it was a Thursday night, the bar had been quiet. Nina had left for the wedding already, a day early, to wrangle her kids and fly up to Auckland.

Tamati, Nina's friend who would be in charge of the bar while we were gone, had been around all day as Tane made sure he had everything he needed. Tamati and Tane were in the back office, so I walked over to the door and locked up after the customers had left. When I turned around, Tane stood next to the bar, arms crossed and watching me. I jumped.

"Jesus. Tane, you scared me."

He raised an eyebrow. "You knew I was here."

"Yes, but not here, here." I gestured with my hand up and down his body and stepped around him. Before I could pass, though, he caught my wrist.

"Can I talk to you?"

I stalled, and looked down at where his fingers gripped me. This was the first time we'd touched in months. He quickly let go.

"Sorry."

"It's okay," I said, looking up and trying to relax. "I'm your fake date, remember? We're going to touch."

He blew out a breath and looked away. "Yeah, about that . . ."

His eyes flicked around the room, looking anywhere but at me.

"Am I still going?" What was going on?

"Yeah, but . . ." He hesitated and then turned, raising an arm to corral me toward the back door. "Come here for a minute."

Tane let me lead, a gentle touch just above the small of my back guiding me. He opened the door and I stepped out onto the back deck. I didn't come out here much, since the servers took care of the food and drinks for guests.

Beyond the squares of light coming through the windows from inside, the deck was in shadows. Tane fumbled for a minute before there was a click and the string lights above me shone down on us. They were warm, casting a soft glow over the entire deck. Wooden chairs and sofas were centered around low tables and fire pits. Beyond the deck, the darkness swallowed up the axe range into mere shadows.

"What's going on?"

Tane stood facing me, his features tense, brow furrowed and arms crossed over his chest. "One thing you should know, since you're an American. We have a greeting."

I raised an eyebrow. "A greeting?"

"Yeah. Some of the women may kiss your cheek, but the traditional way is called a *hongi.* That's how we'll greet the family this weekend. You press your noses"—he gestured between us with his hand—"together. It represents the sharing of life."

"Oh, like a *kunik.*"

Tane shot me a look. "I don't know what that is."

"It's a greeting from the Inuits, where you rub noses."

"We don't rub noses," he said, affronted.

"No, okay, it's similar but not the same. Sorry."

I pictured the move in my mind, and held my hand up to my face. "Is it, like, you bow forward and press noses together?"

He shook his head. "Here, I'll show you." Tane offered me his hand. "This is how you'll greet my family. Handshake, and then lean in."

I slipped my palm into his, a little giddy with the feeling of his big, callused hand in mine. I needed to get used to that this weekend.

Tane bent down, and I was careful not to move too much, lest I headbutt him. This close, in the illumination of the lights, I could see his eyes in such detail, the slight gradient from dark brown on the outer rim to a lighter brown on the inner rim. Our noses and foreheads touched, and I lost my view of his eyes as he closed them.

"Breathe," he said, and I closed my eyes too. Inhale. Exhale. Tane smelled like lemon and tonic. I opened my eyes first, hoping I wasn't being disrespectful, but the view of Tane, blurry from being too close to focus on, was worth it. He looked so serene, calmer than I'd ever seen him with this comfort of his heritage.

The warmth of Tane's skin disappeared from my nose and forehead as he stepped back. "There you go," he said, letting our hands slip apart.

He watched me for a moment while I mentally shook myself out and recovered. Tane's calm had soaked into me.

"I like it," I said when I had found my voice. "It feels spiritual."

"Āe, it does. We've shared breath, and that means something, doesn't it?"

"Yeah," I said softly.

Tane cleared his throat and rubbed his hand over his lips, his attention on my mouth. I looked at his, too. He watched me, his pupils wide, black and bouncing between mine as he took a step closer. "Is this okay?"

He raised a hand and slid his palm around the side of my neck, his fingers pressing into the base of my skull, warm and rough and right where my tattoo was. His pointer finger inched up a bit, through the hair at the nape of my neck, his thumb stroking a line on my tattoo. Tane's eyes flickered down to my lips again.

"Yeah," I said quietly. "It's okay."

Tane stooped—I'd never had a guy stoop to kiss me before—and I closed my eyes. His lips brushed against mine, warm against the crisp night air. Once, twice, and then I breathed out, relaxing against his grip. Tane was gentle with me, soft. Not what I expected from a man built like a tank who was used to throwing rugby players around.

Our lips parted, a bare hint of dampness, and then he backed away. It took a moment for me to open my eyes, and I found him looking out over the range.

"So, yeah . . ." he started, looking anywhere but at me. All the calm feelings from our hongi were replaced with tension, my heart rate speeding up.

"That was good to practice too, right?" I asked, trying to tamp down the nerves that had begun to flutter in my rib cage. "I mean, we will probably kiss in front of your family. It would be weird if we didn't, like, get used to it."

Tane turned back, a small frown on his face. "Practice. Right, that is a good idea."

I touched my lips with my finger, thinking about how odd it was that I missed his already. "Okay, that was a pretty good kiss. Hopefully, it won't be weird when we are around your family." I thought for a moment before chuckling. "If Nina can behave."

Thankfully, Tane laughed with me, which turned into a sigh as he ran his hands over his face. "How did I get myself into this?"

I shrugged. "Nina is just looking out for you, I guess. And you love her."

His hands dropped. "I do. But damn she's crafty as."

TEN

An eight-hour drive to Auckland meant an early morning for me. After our kiss on the back porch, Tane told me that he'd pick me up in his ute—whatever that meant. At six a.m., after only a few hours of sleep, I sat in the lobby of the hostel, waiting. I'd laid my phone on my lap, facedown, expecting the vibration of a text to let me know when he was here.

I must have dozed off, because an indeterminable amount of time later, I was gently shaken awake. I blinked wearily up at

Tane, his big face not far from mine and holding back amusement.

"You snore."

I made a very ladylike noise as I cleared my sinuses, and begged my saliva glands to refill the desert that was my mouth. "Only when I sleep sitting up."

Tane straightened to full height. "So I have that to look forward to all day."

"You're the one who wants to drive. We could be there in an hour," I said, infusing my voice with as much saltiness as I could muster.

"Hey, it's free. Don't be knocking a free trip to Auckland. You could have shelled out the money for a flight."

I sat up as Tane picked up my duffle bag and carried it out the door. I took long strides to catch up to him on the street, where I found his big truck idling at the curb. I opened the door and climbed into the passenger seat. "You promised me a nap—let's go."

The truck—ute—bounced as my bag joined his in the truck bed, and then Tane climbed into the driver's side.

We pulled away and I watched Wellington outside my window, the city waking up. Either because of my little nap in the lobby, or because I was in a car with Tane, sleep eluded me.

I rolled my head over on the headrest to look at Tane. "So, we never talked about who's getting married."

Tane told me about the family, the bride and groom and all the extended relatives visiting. He became more animated as we talked, excited to see them. It sounded like it had been a while since they'd had the whole family together.

It was cute, and Tane's smile as he talked about his family made him seem younger, and I tried to picture what Tane had looked like as a kid.

The names of his relatives were often complicated, and I repeated some of them back to Tane to make sure I had them right. Tane's excitement kept him talking, and while he talked about his aunts, I closed my eyes and then dropped off to sleep.

Sometime later I blinked awake and stretched. Rolling hillsides were passing by out my window, idyllically dotted with sheep and slashed with fence lines. Tane was staring straight ahead, his big, blunt fingers tapping on the steering wheel to the music quietly playing on the radio. He looked pretty serene for a guy who'd been cooped up in a car all morning.

Tane caught me watching him and smiled, his dark eyes dancing in the daylight with an incoming tease. "You do snore when you sleep upright."

I didn't blink at him. "I bet you snore too. That nose of yours looks mangled from the outside; I bet the inside is a labyrinth."

Tane laughed.

"Sorry I fell asleep. Where are we?"

"Outside Palmerston North," he said, right as a sign hurled past my window declaring the exact same thing. Not that that told me anything, actually, since I had no idea where Palmerston North was. Or Palmerston South, for that matter. Any of the Palmerstons.

"It's pretty."

"Yeah, mate. Good country."

A quick glance at the dash told me it had only been an hour and a half. I turned to face Tane again. "So you told your mom you were seeing someone?"

He sighed. "Yeah, a couple of months ago. She loves me, but she's a bit fixated on me settling down."

"And that got her to leave you alone?"

He rolled his eyes in exasperation. "I thought she'd back off once she knew I was dating someone, but it got worse! She wanted to know how I met you, what your name was, what *iwi* you belonged to—"

"Iwi?" I cut him off.

"Family, or tribe."

"Does it matter that I'm not Māori? Or from your iwi?"

"Nah." Tane waved off my concern. "The groom is white too. Mum's just happy I'm with someone."

"Okay, so what does she know?"

"You mean what did she wrestle out of me?" He grinned. "We met at the bar. She knows your name is Claire," he said, and I think he was blushing. "Mum gave me hell when she found out your place card was going to say 'guest.' So I called as soon as you agreed, and told her."

"So not much about me, then? I don't have to pretend to be someone else?"

"Nah." He shook his head, shifting in his seat. "Better to stick with the truth, hey?"

We sat in silence for a little while, me watching for signs of the town and Tane steadfastly driving.

A few minutes later we passed a sign that pointed off to the right for the New Zealand Rugby Museum. "Hey, there's a museum? Are you in it?"

I looked back at Tane just in time to see the muscles in his jaw tick. "Yeah. Everyone is."

"Is your sister?"

"No." His eyebrows drew together.

"Your mom."

That earned me an eye roll. "No."

"Well, then, you, sir, must be a pretty big fucking deal."

"Every rugby player for New Zealand is in it, Claire."

"Oh. So it's not like a hall of fame?"

"Nah. Just about the game."

"Have you visited? As a tourist, I mean."

"No."

"Why not?"

Tane gave me side-eye. "You really just needed a power nap, didn't ya? Made you chatty."

"Better than mainlining coffee," I said, nodding toward his giant empty travel mug sitting between us.

"How'd a morning person like you end up working at a bar, then?"

"Necessity. You make good money working at bars. Especially girls," I said. Especially girls like me. Pretty enough to draw attention and get good tips.

He grunted.

"What about you? Why did you play rugby?"

He sighed and pushed his head back into the headrest. "The usual reasons: money, fame, girls. I was good at it."

The unspoken end hovered above our heads. *But I'm not good at it now.*

Instead of lamenting his forced hand, he changed the subject. "What's the story behind the tattoo on the back of your neck?"

"Oh." Self-consciously, I moved my hand back to cover the tattoo. "It's an icosahedron, a D20 dice."

"Yes, I am familiar with it."

"You are?" I said, surprised.

He snorted. "We have Dungeons & Dragons here, you know."

"Right, well. That's why I have it."

"Do you play?"

"Not anymore. I got the tattoo when I turned eighteen and I still played with my friends."

"But you used to?"

"Yeah." A thought occurred to me. "Should I cover up my tattoo for the wedding? I can go get some concealer in Auckland tomorrow."

At that, Tane laughed. "Woman, look at me. My whole family is tattooed just as much as I am. Well, most of them," he amended. "You'll be fine."

"Your tattoos are mostly hidden. If I had long hair, no one could see it, but it'll be on display in my dress."

"Don't worry about it. A few of my family even have *moko kauae*—traditional face tattoos," he filled in at my questioning glance. "Your D20 is fine."

"Good."

"So why don't you play anymore? I bet there's some groups you could join in Welly. I'd imagine they'd love to have a pretty girl."

I bristled. "Yes, exactly why I want to be accepted into a group of dudes playing D&D."

Tane shifted to look at me better. "You don't like compliments very much, do you?"

I glared at him.

"Oh, actually." He rubbed his chin. "It's only when they compliment your looks. I've seen you hit on enough to know that's the worst thing they could say. You love it when your cocktails get compliments. Your face gets all flushed and you grin like a kid."

"Do not."

"Why don't you like compliments, Claire?"

"None of your business, *sir*," I bit out.

We rode in silence for several miles, and I picked up my phone to check it for the first time since we'd gotten into the car. I had a flood of messages from Iris, but with my phone still on do not disturb, I hadn't gotten the buzzes.

Iris: You drive up to Auckland today, right?

Iris: How big is Auckland anyway?

Iris: Wait, how big is Wellington?

Iris: Google says just over a million and a half in Auckland. That's New Zealand's biggest city! CLAIRE. THAT'S TINY.

Iris: Oh, are you going to go to the waterfront?

Iris: You know they have a wine island?

Iris: CLAIRE!!! Did you wake up in time?

I smiled at my sister's texts and checked the global clock on my phone. Afternoon in Chicago.

Me: I'm alive. I'm on the road. Calm your tits.

Iris: You're in the car with Tane?

Me: Yes. We are on time, yes, Auckland is bigger than Wellington, and they are both tiny. I read her texts again.

Me: What's the wine island?

Iris: It's called Waiheke, and it's a short ferry ride away. You should totally go!

Me: No time. We have the rehearsal dinner tonight and then Tane's going to be gone most of the day tomorrow and then we have the wedding.

Iris: You should go by yourself.

*Me: *gasp* What's this? Iris encouraging me to go do things . . . alone.*

Iris: You made it all the way to New Zealand by yourself. I'm so proud of you.

Me: I couldn't have done it without you. I smiled and changed the subject. *How's Chris?*

Iris: Fine. Fine. Working a lot. Babe, gotta go, one last meeting today. XO

I sighed and leaned my head back against the headrest.

Tane had been quiet since I'd shut down our conversation. Without the phone to distract me, I tapped a nail on the door handle to my left.

"You don't like talking about your rugby career. How is that different?"

Tane threw a glare at me before turning to face ahead again. "What, you want a quid pro quo? Fine, my rugby career was taken away from me after a bad tackle and now I'm just a fat fucker who drinks too much. Your turn."

His bitterness flooded the car, crawling into my senses; I could smell it, taste it.

"Used to," I said.

"What?" He glanced at me, eyebrows scrunched up.

"You used to drink too much."

He did a double take, eyes on the road and back to me, back to the road and back to me.

His face softened, shoulders dropping an inch or two.

"It wasn't that long ago that I gave it up."

I shrugged. "Doesn't make it any less true. You used to drink too much."

He nodded, looking thoughtful, and I watched the road pass by outside for a while.

"I had a group of friends," I started, "that I played D&D with. Like, when I was thirteen, there were six of us. We met in the back of one kid's parents' bar. It was probably, like, a mobster spot or something for illegal gambling, but they let us use it on Saturday mornings."

He said nothing, just nodded in acknowledgment.

"It was all guys, of course. And I was a stick prepuberty. You know, unlike my voluptuous curves today," I said, gesturing at my flat chest.

Tane glanced over. "Curves don't make women sexy, Claire. Women make themselves sexy."

I flushed, even though his perusal was quick. "Well, whatever. I grew up playing games with a bunch of boys who basically looked like me but with acne and crooked teeth and then braces and changing voices. They were my best friends, but we started to grow up. And people change."

I looked out the window at the two-lane highway, the occasional car coming by. We were out in the middle of nowhere, rural New Zealand.

"Do you still keep in touch with them?" he asked me.

"No."

"What happened?"

It took a few breaths for me to get the words out. I hated how they always sounded, conceited, even if I wished everything were different. "There was one guy in our group. He was my best friend. We had, like, no parental supervision and we'd thought it was so cool of our parents."

I stared at the road ahead, remembering the good times. Others in our game lamented about things like curfews and having to keep their bedroom door open. We played our own games, staying up late at night, hardly spending time apart.

"But it was like a switch was flipped one day for him. I was no longer his best friend. I was a girl. I was an easy target for him. We spent all our time together anyway—what was a kiss here or a touch there?"

I glanced over at Tane, watching for reactions, but he was silent, staring out the windshield and flexing his hands on the steering wheel.

"I was a stupid teenager, and so confused, and when I complained, my parents said, 'Boys will be boys.' They'd barely been parental figures when I was a kid; it just got worse after I graduated high school. That's when Devon really started getting bad." I paused, gathering up my thoughts. "He started talking about plans for us, like we'd move in together, and I had no say in it. He said I owed him. Like he'd put up with me for years, been my best friend just so that when I got 'hot'"—I air-quoted the words—"he'd get to sleep with me."

Tane stroked his face, keeping his eyes on the road, but his jaw was tense. It felt delicate, unintrusive, when he finally asked, "How bad did it get?"

"I never slept with him. But it scared me. One time he got me alone and pushed me up against the wall of an alley. I—I don't know what would have happened if a coworker hadn't interrupted us." I took a deep breath and Tane let me gather myself.

"It took us years—and some help from a lawyer friend of Iris's—to get a restraining order. Devon would hang around for a while, disrupt my job and get violent with anyone he thought I was dating, whether I was or not. Then he'd disappear again. Every time, I'd think maybe he was finally gone for real. But he always popped back up. Anyway, that's one reason I decided to come to New Zealand. I needed a change of scenery, and he doesn't know I'm here. He wouldn't think to look for me here." I turned my attention out the window, feeling too fragile to see Tane's reaction.

"I'm sorry, Claire."

"Thank you. So, yeah, I hate it when people compliment my looks."

We fell quiet, both of us lost, I suspected, in our pasts.

ELEVEN

A knock resounded through my hotel room; Tane was right on time.

I smoothed my button-down and grabbed my purse before answering the door. We'd checked into our separate rooms with an hour to kill before we had to leave for the rehearsal dinner.

"What happened to your T-shirt?" Tane blurted when I opened the door.

"I changed." I looked down at myself. Instead of the pajama bottoms and T-shirt I'd worn in the car, I was wearing jeans and ankle boots and the nicest top I had—one of the black button-downs from the bar.

"You look like you're going to work. Change back into the T-shirt."

"It's the nicest thing I have!"

He gestured at himself, wearing cargo shorts and a threadbare T-shirt. "I'm not your fucking boss right now."

"I'm meeting your family."

"They're all going to be wearing togs and T-shirts. Change . . . please."

I rolled my eyes and slammed the door in his face. Two minutes later I was out in the hall, wearing a T-shirt that said "Chaotic Neutral" across the front.

Tane dipped his chin. "Better, let's go."

"Geez," I grumbled. "Way to make me feel comfortable, sir."

He shot me a look. "Are you nervous?" he taunted, and I stuck my tongue out.

The rehearsal dinner party was at the bride's parents' house, Tane's aunt and uncle, who lived out in the 'burbs. When we arrived at the two-story brick home, Tane led me to the side and paused with his hand on the gate. He held his hand out, palm up. "You ready?"

I slid my fingers into his, my thin ones sliding between his beefy ones. He tapped my ring, a thick silver band with engraved vines along it, three times with his thumb. Then he swung the gate open with one hand and pulled me close with our interlocked hands.

To my surprise, he kissed me right then and there as a cheer went up from the backyard. A quick peck and a rapscallion grin before tugging me in with him.

And yes, I was fine. Tane and Nina's family was on par with my expectations: teasing for Tane; warm, friendly smiles for me; and generous hugs. Tane led me around, introducing me to his family as his girlfriend. There was a lot—and I mean *a lot*—of rugby talk.

Nina and her family were there, the girls running around with similar-aged cousins and Hemi talking to a group of guys by the grill. Our greetings were brief; there were lots of people around.

"Where's your mom?" I asked Nina.

"She's on the committee of mums who are finishing the decorations. You'll meet her tomorrow."

As soon as his family heard my accent, they peppered me with questions. Tane and I got separated into different conversations, but I could feel his eyes on me. When I glanced over anytime I could, Tane's eyebrow would rise. *Just checking in: Do you need a rescue?*

I realized, then, that I hadn't really been around that many locals. The hostel was full of foreigners and when I socialized with my coworkers, they were usually the working-holiday-visa ones. The Kiwis I worked with dispersed back to their homes and families at the end of the night.

We ate from the grill as I tried to answer questions on topics I knew nearly nothing about, such as gerrymandering and foreign policy. Who knew that this was why I should have paid attention in history class, to impress my fake Kiwi boyfriend's family? But they were either impressed or amused by American politics, so I seemed to be doing a decent job of remembering things.

I had finished my dinner by the time Tane had broken away from conversation to get his own plate. He straddled the bench beside me, resting a hand on my shoulder and squeezing, kissing my temple. After an hour or so talking to strangers, the familiarity of his hand relaxed me. He shifted toward my ear, his breath ghosting over my cheek.

"Are you doing okay?"

"Yeah, thanks," I said. "Your family"—I waved around to encompass everyone—"is pretty great."

Tane grunted and picked up a thick stack of burgers—they put odd things on their burgers here. Even McDonald's had a Kiwiburger with fried egg and beet slices on it. His knee pressed up against the side of my thigh.

"So, Claire, what have you been doing here in New Zealand?" Tane's uncle Matt—the father of the bride—asked me.

I crossed my arms and rested my elbows on the picnic table. "Honestly, not much. I've been saving up my money a little bit to try to get a car. What do you think I should see?"

That led to a fiery discussion that required little input from me. I loved how passionate Kiwis were about their country. When Tane finished eating, he dropped his napkin onto his plate and dusted his hands off before sliding them around me, tugging me into the V of his thighs.

Some of his family noticed the affection and exchanged smiles. Tane was good at this, and I tried to relax more into him. He was warm and comfortable.

"The ferry's crazy expensive, mate," he argued with one of his cousins. "And it's getting too cold anyway. Not worth going down to Wanaka, if you ask me."

I snorted. "Please, I'm from Boston. I can handle some cold." Although, I hadn't packed my cold-weather gear. I was going to need to buy more, based on how bitter the wind was whipping around Wellington.

"Hey, Tane," a voice called, and out of the corner of my eye something flew toward us. Tane snatched it out of the air before it could hit me.

A few gasps went up and Tane shifted protectively under me.

"Still got those rugby reflexes, then," a young man said. I couldn't remember if I'd been introduced to him yet. The names and faces were starting to blend together a bit, but this guy was young, maybe still a teenager. The woman next to him—his sister?—glared at him.

"Oi, Park. Careful there. My catch is better than your aim, but someday I won't be fast enough." Tension around the backyard eased, and a few other people threw jabs at Park's throwing skills.

The thing in Tane's hand was a beer bottle. Just like that, I saw beer bottles everywhere. Everyone was drinking but Tane.

My eyes caught Nina's. She watched Tane, brow crinkled and concern etching her features. I wondered how many of the family knew that Tane was sober now.

Everyone was still laughing over the ribbings and Tane placed the beer, unopened, on the table. We glanced at each other, and he gave me a small, tentative smile, leaning in. "I shoulda brought my own, hey?"

If his family noticed the unopened beer, they didn't say anything.

TWELVE

Tane was busy with wedding errands,
helping out the bride—his cousin—and
his mom. I took the bus in Auckland armed with
a list of suggestions from my friends on what to
do. I scoped out the war museum, the botanical
gardens, and a nice public green space called
the Auckland Domain, which reminded me a bit
of Central Park, with museums and trails and
sports fields. I enjoyed myself a bit too much
and had to rush back to the hotel to shower and
get ready for the wedding.

This time, I checked with Nina to make sure my outfit was appropriate, sending her a pic of me in my dress. The wedding was in a hotel ballroom, but based on how casual everyone had been the night before, I wanted to be sure.

When I opened the door at Tane's arrival, I expected some sort of ribbing about my outfit, but he was oddly quiet.

The door clicked closed, and I gestured. "Better today, right?"

He put his hands into his pockets and we scanned each other. Tane was in a pin-striped gray suit that had to have been custom-made. No way would his thighs fit in anything off the rack. A dark blue handkerchief peeking out of his pocket drew my eye.

I tried to think back—had I ever seen Tane like this? He didn't dress up around the bar, sticking with athletic gear.

"Fishing for compliments?"

"No, sir, proper attire checking only."

He scanned me again, from the black-and-tan floral pattern to the ankle boots and then back up to my hair, which, since it was getting a little longer, I had styled.

"Hideous," he said, clicking his tongue and shaking his head. "But the dress looks nice."

I stuck my tongue out and flipped him off. He didn't move, so I paused, waiting for him. To my surprise, he leaned forward, clasping a hand on my waist, and even though we were alone in the hallway, no one to see a kiss for a fake date, he brushed his lips against mine ever so gently. My lips parted in surprise, and I sucked in a breath, but Tane moved back before I could react further. My body tightened, thinking about that kiss under the sky on the back porch and now this. We were edging outside of the expectations I had for this trip, but I didn't mind those lines being crossed.

In fact, I might be liking it too much.

"Thanks for doing this, Claire," he said softly, oblivious to my thoughts.

I swallowed, wondering how he could match my temper so well sometimes but yet flip it around on a dime other times, turning everything sweet.

He offered me his elbow, and we rode the elevator down to the ballroom, where guests were crowding around the hallway. Some faces I remembered from the night before, but most were new. We dropped our linked hands to hongi with the family, but Tane's hand always returned to the small of my back afterward.

"And this is my mum, Emily," Tane said.

Mrs. Taumata and I did a hongi together, and when she released me, she pinched Tane's cheek and teased him.

I looked more closely at her. Even if we hadn't been introduced, I would have known her as Tane's mother. She and Nina could have been sisters. Emily was wearing a flowing navy dress paired with a cropped jacket.

When she met my eyes, we smiled at each other.

"You're going to sit with Mum and Nina while I do my usher thing if that's okay?" Tane asked me.

"Sure," I said. Tane was handed a stack of programs, and he offered me one elbow, his mom the other. "Ready, ladies?"

The doors were open and a queue was forming, people waiting for the ushers to lead them to their seats. We cut the line and stepped into the ballroom. It was . . . very pink. Gauzy white fabric swept over the walls and ceilings, tied off with satin pink ribbons and massive arrangements of pink and white flowers.

Tane led us to our assigned seats and made sure his mom was settled before he strode back to the doors.

"Claire," Mrs. Taumata said, leaning toward me and placing a palm on the empty chair between us, Tane's seat when his job was done. "I am so glad you are here."

"Thank you, Mrs. Taumata." I threaded my fingers together in my lap, feeling a little bad for hoodwinking the family.

"Please, call me Emily." She placed a hand on mine, her brown skin a contrast against my own. "I was worried about him, you know. He was too flashy. And also, not happy. I tried to tell him not to do the bar, but a mother can only do so much. I want what's best for him."

"I do too."

"Good. He needs a stable life. A family of his own." She winked at me. "Soon."

Oh Jesus. Someone get me my birth control pills.

Thankfully, we were interrupted by Tane arriving with Nina, Hemi trailing behind. Tane and Nina were bickering. "Why do you have to show me to my seat? I'm not an old lady who can't figure it out. No offense, Mum."

"None taken."

"It's my job, Nina. Don't piss off the bride, yeah?"

"I wouldn't dream. But I'll gladly piss you off. You're the one who thought it would be a good idea to tell Uncle James that the rumor was true and your loose forward had, in fact, cheated on his wife. Seriously, you made the man cry."

Tane rolled his eyes and mumbled a curse, practically pushing his sister toward me before stalking down the aisle.

Emily swatted her daughter as she passed us to take her seat. "You know James wants his kid to play rugby. Don't make everyone out to be so bad."

Nina fanned herself with a wedding program and turned to me as we both made room for Hemi to get by. She placed a hand on my arm, squeezing it. "My family's not so bad, eh? And Tane's being good to you, yes?"

I assured her that he was. "Where are the girls?"

"One of Mum's friends is watching them so we can have a date night," Nina said as she nudged Hemi. Nina and Emily chatted, catching up on local and family gossip. Hemi seemed perfectly happy staying out of the conversation. In fact, he had never said much around me at all, seeming to prefer being around his kids than other adults.

It was a stark contrast to bubbly and social Nina, who'd never met a person she didn't like and talked like it was her job.

Well, different strokes for different folks.

It took a while for everyone to get settled in, with stragglers arriving in a rush to make the ceremony. Finally the music paused and Tane stepped around his mother to sit beside me.

He laced his fingers through mine, seemingly without thinking about it. On his other side, his hand interlocked with his mother's and then Nina grabbed my hand too, giving it a squeeze.

What a family. My heart clenched in a sudden longing for my sister, the only true family I had, thousands of miles away.

THIRTEEN

The ceremony was beautiful, given in both English and Māori, and Emily and Nina readily had their tissues out to wipe tears of joy and blow their noses. At one point, Tane sniffed next to me. Our eyes caught, and before I could stop it, a slow smile spread across my face. He rolled his eyes and nudged me, but I squeezed his hand and he squeezed back.

And then his thumb started to slowly stroke over the back of my hand. I looked down, only half paying attention to the vows. Tane's thick, blunt fingers tangled with my slim ones, his rough calluses running over the fine bones.

When I looked up again, he was focused on the ceremony. But the stroking didn't stop.

The chain finally broke when the couple was declared husband and wife, and we all stood up to clap. Immediately I missed the warmth of Tane's hand, but it soon moved to the small of my back as he led me out of the hall.

Next were the photographs, where Tane and his family were stolen away for a huge family photo. I wandered around with a glass of champagne, admiring pictures of the bride and groom. There were family photos—the bride with her parents, a slim pale woman with curly gray hair and a wiry bald man covered with traditional tattoos— and photos of the couple together with a border collie.

"Claire." Nina came up behind me and tugged on my elbow. "Come with me."

I followed her, threading through the crowd that was building by the dance floor. "Where are we going?"

Her hand slipped down to mine to keep us together. "It's time for the haka."

"What's the haka?"

The crowd grew unnaturally still, and that was when the shouting started. Nina was still weaving us through to the far edge, trying to find a place where we could see.

The single voice, harsh and strained, echoed off the vaulted ceilings of the ballroom, building to a crescendo. The words were in Māori, and the echoing call came just as we reached the edge of the crowd.

A dozen men, Māori and white, many of them from the wedding party, stood huddled together. Suit jackets were discarded, sleeves rolled up. My eyes snapped to Tane, the tallest of the group.

At the collective shout, the men started to spread out, a low growl resounding. There was more shouting—raw, primal screams—and the group faced the bride and groom, who stood together, watching.

Tane was near us, the edge of the group, and I could see his profile—it was the only thing I could focus on. How could I look away?

His eyes were wide, cheeks puffed out. Tane distorted his face into something fearsome. Tongue out, eyes wide, his feet were planted firmly, his weight sunk low. He, and the men on the edges of my vision, bounced lightly.

"This," Nina whispered to me, "is the haka. This is our shout to the gods, our war cry, our way to remember our culture."

There was a call from the back, and as one, the men slapped their thighs. They shouted, stamped their feet, slapped their chests, moved together.

Nina let go of my hand, and I turned my head, catching sight of the bride and groom. They had both joined in, the haunting calls and the rhythm of the slapping forming a song. The bride, tears streaming down her face, black hair pulled back into an intricate design and lace over her tattoo-covered shoulders, shouted and slapped alongside her new husband.

My vision went blurry and I quickly wiped tears from my eyes. It was just so *moving*.

And quietly, it was over. No applause, no fanfare, just the newlyweds slipping from one person to another, clasping hands and exchanging hongi.

Tane pressed his nose and forehead to the bride's and then the groom's, and made his way to us. He and Nina did the hongi together, and then hugged. His shirt was damp with sweat, and he was still breathing hard.

"Claire," he said, offering his hand to me. I slid my palm against his, our thumbs intertwining. Instead of letting him guide me, this time I cupped the back of his neck with my hand, guiding us both as we pressed our forehead and nose together.

We took a breath, and Tane brushed his lips against mine before pulling back.

After the haka, we ate. We sat with some of Tane's cousins, around his age, with spouses or partners. After introductions were made, Tane mentioned I'd been on my own in Auckland today.

"Do anything good?" his cousin Ari asked. He had glasses and dark curly hair and was dressed in a suit a size too big for him.

"Tane had suggested the Domain, since I only had a day. I walked around the botanical gardens and toured the Auckland War Memorial Museum."

"Yeah, good call," said Ari's girlfriend, Jill. "Ari's played a few pickup games there, and we went to a concert in the Wintergardens once, didn't we?"

The conversation shifted around as they reminisced and shared stories while I listened. Even though he was absorbed with his family, Tane kept touching me. A squeeze on my thigh, a hand on my back between courses. It was like he'd given himself permission, was really playing the game. Like I actually was his girlfriend.

A silly thing to think about, obviously. This was fake. I was his employee. And in a few months, I wouldn't even be that anymore. I'd be somewhere else, and then it'd be time to go home to Boston.

Jill leaned over to me. It was after the main course and we were waiting for the dancing to start, Tane talking to his neighbor about the latest political scandal of which I had no knowledge.

"You have an audience," Jill said. When I looked at her, she flicked her eyes to her right. "That's Tane's mum and sister, right?"

I took a sip from my glass, trying to look inconspicuous. Yes, Jill was right: Nina and Emily were staring at us from the next table over.

When I made eye contact with Nina, she and her mother both turned back to each other.

I leaned over toward Tane, resting my chin on his shoulder, and when he finished his sentence, he turned to look at me, blocking his family from my sight.

"Does your mom know this is a fake date?" I whispered right in his ear.

"No, why?"

"I think Nina and your mom are in cahoots."

Tane looked at them too, but they were busy talking to each other now, trying too hard not to look at us, I thought.

Just then the volume of the music went up.

"Allllll right, ladies and gentlemen, it's time to hit the dance floor. Blake and Aroha are leading the way."

"Well, then," Tane said, pushing back his seat and standing up. "Let's give them something to cahoot about."

I laughed as Tane stripped off his jacket and tie. "Jill, Ari, you coming?"

Tane rolled his sleeves up—hello, forearms—while the rest of the men at the table followed suit, and then he led me out to the dance floor.

———

Hours later we'd had dessert, danced more, and then Tane went back for another piece of cake while I spent some time off my feet.

"This is a really fun party," I said, watching Tane shovel white frosted cake into his mouth by the forkful. He'd unbuttoned his shirt a bit more, showing off a peek of a tattoo on his chest and more tanned skin.

"You sure you don't want more cake?" he asked between bites.

"Nah, thanks. It's so sweet, it made my teeth hurt."

Tane took the last bite and set the plate down, licking icing from his thumbs—how had he gotten icing everywhere?

Fake date, I thought as I watched his tongue a little too closely.

The music had been loud dance music for the most part, so we slipped back into the crowd. Nina was easy to find, and we all danced together for a few songs.

Then the beat shifted to a slow song. I swear, Nina looked like she wanted to push us together, but Tane moved before she did, slipping his hands around my waist.

My arms were already moving up to his neck as he bent down to whisper in my ear, "Dance with me."

I pressed in close, twining my fingers together behind his head. With Tane's height, I was just about eye level with the bare skin in the V of his shirt.

"Sorry I'm so sweaty," he said.

His shirt was damp under my wrists, and beads of sweat had formed on his temples. "I don't mind," I assured him. "And you smell good."

At that, Tane turned his head, kissing the soft skin on the inside of my elbow. The hairs on my arm rose, my stomach flipping.

I cleared my throat. The gesture had been so intimate, so tender. It was hard to remember that this wasn't a real relationship. "Your mom watching?"

Tane didn't even look around, his voice hoarse and low in my ear. "Yeah."

We swayed together, and it was nice. It was nice to catch our breath, nice to have a quieter moment without the loud pumping bass, nice to have nothing to look at but Tane.

Nice to have the press of Tane's body against mine, the warmth of him infusing the air around us.

Maybe it was more than nice. I licked my lips, and my attention wandered to the places we touched. I let my hand slide down along his shirt collar, let the edge slip between my two fingers. Accidentally, the pad of my finger brushed over his skin. This was the tattooed side, where geometric shapes swirled. I didn't look up to see his face, but I heard a sharp inhale of breath as goose bumps covered the skin I could see.

Goddamn, I wanted to see the rest of the tattoo.

The song ended, the music shifting back to an upbeat song, and I let the tension go. Tane bent his head toward my ear. "Ready to go?"

"We can stay longer if you want," I offered.

"Nah, we've been dancing awhile and, maybe it's because I'm not drinking, but I'm getting tired." I hadn't had much to drink either, just two glasses of bubbles.

I nodded and Tane tugged me out of the dancing crowd and back to our table. We made the rounds to say goodbye and within ten minutes were in the elevator zooming back up to the rooms.

Tane leaned his head against the wall opposite me and caught my eye, a smile slipping over his lips. The space between us felt forced now. This wasn't right—he shouldn't be all the way over there. I wanted him all the way over here.

My eyes drifted down to the open collar of his shirt, the beads of sweat cooling on his skin. His suit jacket was draped over his forearm, the tie held loosely in his hand.

Okay, the sexual tension was getting to me, because right then I really wanted to climb Tane and rub myself all over him.

I was sex-deprived. Obviously. And overstimulated. When was the last time I'd had sex? I did some mental math while the elevator whisked us up. One year and six months, give or take a week or two.

I nearly shuddered. Thank God for vibrators. Granted, since I'd packed light for New Zealand, I had only that small bullet, which was, stupidly, back in the hostel in Wellington.

While thinking, my eyes had wandered back up to Tane's. And as if he knew what I was thinking, they were full of heat and intensity.

I clenched.

Goddamn it. I was going to sleep with my boss.

"Claire?" Tane pushed off the wall and his hand touched the small of my back for the millionth time today. I realized the door was open and he was waiting on me to exit.

"Sorry," I said, quickly stepping out and pausing while I tried to remember where my room was. An awkward second later I turned right and strode down the hall, taking a deep breath and trying to get my head back on straight.

We stopped at my door and I fumbled with the key card. The light flashed green and I cracked the door open, turning back to Tane. He stood, arms crossed, an intense look on his face.

"What?" I asked.

"I'm wondering how terrible of an idea it would be to kiss you again."

My breath caught in my throat. "The other times weren't terrible ideas?"

"They were practice. This would be real." He shifted on his feet, a quick break in eye contact. "I'm your boss. And I wasn't sure if you—" I shut him up. Or, I tried to, anyway. With one hand yanking him by the front of his shirt, and the other on the back of his neck, pulling him down, I got his attention.

Maybe it was because our kisses had been light and gentle up to this point, but this one was decidedly *not.* Tane's mouth opened over mine, his tongue invading, his body crowding me until I was pressed up against the doorjamb. He tasted of salt and sugar and heat.

His hands came up to either side of my neck, thumbs pressing gently into the soft skin of my chin and tilting my head up farther. His fingertips splayed as he groaned and pressed harder, kissed fiercer.

Until he disappeared, a full step away before I could even open my eyes. He swallowed audibly and averted his eyes. His chest rose and fell, his breath coming hard as he licked his lips. Tane cleared his throat, and for a half a second I was ready to invite him in.

But he turned away before I could open my mouth. "Good night, Claire."

I was left panting and gasping, watching him walk into his room three doors down.

What the hell?

FOURTEEN

I slept like shit. Vigorously rubbing myself last night hadn't been successful and I deeply regretted leaving my vibrator in Wellington. What the fuck had I been thinking? Spending a weekend with a hot man, dancing, kissing. No shit I'd be horny.

Gah.

Despite the closed curtains, light was beginning to creep in and I knew I'd have to eventually get up, give up on sleep and hating on my own body, and find food.

And Tane. He needed to explain what was going on inside his head, but whatever it was, I didn't think I was going to like it. Perhaps in my flustered physical state, I was a little angrier than I should have been. I was sure Tane thought he was being a gentleman, taking it slow. He probably also thought I'd gotten myself off last night. In fact, he'd probably gotten himself off. Lucky bastard.

But I was not here to take it slow. I had a little more than two months left working for him, and then I'd be leaving the bar, hopefully with a great recommendation from Nina. There was no taking it slow. Taking it slow meant, like . . . dating.

I wasn't interested in dating, especially when I would be back in Boston before the end of the year.

Unfortunately, our morning was booked with a brunch with Tane and Nina's mother. The lobby of the hotel was no place to tell someone that you wanted bangifits, so I thanked Tane for my to-go coffee and trailed after him to the parking lot. A few minutes into our drive, Nina called with some kind of family-logistics crisis, so I sipped my coffee in silence as I listened to Tane's one-sided conversation. When we pulled into the driveway of his family home, the front door opened and Emily waved to us. Tane pulled the phone away from his mouth. "Do you mind going in? I might have to go take some cousins to the airport."

I made a face. "Just me and your mom?"

He shot me a grin. "No worries, my mum loves you."

I got out of the car and tried to look excited to be alone with Tane and Nina's mom.

"Claire!" Emily wrapped me up in a big hug. "I'm so glad you could join us for brunch, too. Where's Tane going?"

I turned around to find Tane's truck backing out of the driveway. He held up his hand and mouthed, *Five minutes*.

I stuck my tongue out at him, pretty sure it was bad form to leave your girlfriend—even a fake one—with your mother when they'd only met the previous day. But thankfully, it was Emily, and she'd been pretty awesome so far—even with the pressure to pop out grandbabies way too soon. If I were a real girlfriend, I'd have some opinions to give on that.

But for now, I turned back to Emily. "He and Nina have had to shuffle some errands around. I think she's running late." I stepped into the entryway of their home and looked around.

"You know," Emily said with a sparkle in her eye, "I've got some baby photos of Tane to show you, if you're interested."

I perked up. "And maybe some embarrassing stories?"

Emily chuckled. "Oh, so many. Let me pull out the photo albums!"

A few minutes later I was sitting on the floor of the living room with five photo albums spread out around me. The room was a relic to Tane's and Nina's lives. Photos of them both hung everywhere, but I paid extra attention to Tane's. His life was documented from baby photos to youth rugby to professional team photos. Family photos showed the two of them with a much-younger Emily and a large, gruff-looking man, a spitting image of Tane.

When the man himself finally walked in, followed closely behind by Nina and her family, Emily got up to kiss and hug everyone—grandkids first—and Tane got a good look at the photo album on the floor.

His eyes bugged out. "Mum! You're showing her the naked baby photos?"

Emily swatted her son. "It's nothing she hasn't seen before."

I held up the photo in question. "You were so small, Tane. Look at that little thing."

He rolled his eyes and huffed good-humoredly, bending down to give me a quick peck on the lips. Nina cackled behind him.

"Don't be too smug," I told her. "I've already seen the pictures of you after your at-home haircut."

"Mum," Nina whined.

"It's your fault—you're late. If you'd been here on time, we would be eating and not killing time by looking at pictures."

"Well, then technically, it's Nora's fault. She's the one whose nappy exploded on me." Hemi bounced the toddler on his hip.

The albums were abandoned as we moved toward the kitchen. Emily gave us all jobs and directed me and Hemi to pull dishes out of the warm oven while Tane and Nina set the table and a full English breakfast was laid out.

Everyone paused while Emily said a quick blessing in Māori and then we dug in. Tane was back to playing the dutiful boyfriend, but now, with last night's kiss between us, he was even more affectionate. I felt myself falling back into the comfort of the kisses and touches and it was all too easy. I was happy to keep up the ruse for Emily, but I tried to remind myself that we needed to have the Talk.

"How is the bar doing?" Emily asked at one point. The question made me realize how good of a job Tane and Nina had done keeping their family life separate from their work life. There had been no talk of the bar the entire weekend.

"Good," Nina told her. "Claire's even been helping us by introducing a new cocktail menu. She's talented."

I flushed under the compliment and Tane's hand wandered over to my thigh, giving my jean-clad knee a quick squeeze.

"They are really good," Hemi agreed.

I stared at him. "When did you come and have one and why didn't I get to serve it to you personally?"

He shrugged. "Sometimes we hire a babysitter and have a lunch date. It hasn't worked with your schedule, I guess."

"It's a shame we are going to lose her in a couple months," Nina added.

Emily gasped. "What? Why?"

"Mum, Claire's on a working holiday visa. She has to get a new job after six months with us."

"Pish. That's ridiculous. Just marry her already."

Tane and I both choked on our food. Nina snorted. Hemi didn't even bother looking up from feeding Nora.

"Mum, you know it's more complicated than that," Tane chided her.

Yeah, that *was the problem with her suggestion?*

Fortunately, Nina changed the subject—mirth in her eyes as she saved us—and before I knew it,

I was full and sleepy, pushing back from the table and trying not to yawn.

We counteracted food comas with tea, coffee, and conversation until Nina's kids got restless and she checked the time. "Okay, Mum, we've got to go catch our flight. Wrangling these kids is going to be difficult."

"Oh wait, before you go, can you look at the gutter in the back?"

"I nominate Tane. He and Claire only have a couple hours' drive to Matamata today." With that, Nina gathered her things—husband and kids included—and said her goodbyes. When the door closed behind them, Tane and Emily went out the back door and looked at the gutters. I made myself useful washing dishes by hand. When they were all clean, I dried and stacked and then wandered back to the photo albums.

Looking at them made me a little sad. I wasn't sure Iris and I had enough photos of us as kids to fill one album, never mind the half a dozen that I could see.

I snapped a picture of the albums spread open and messaged her.

Do we have any family photo albums?

She didn't answer right away, so I was still flipping through the albums when Tane and Emily came back in, talking about repair work to the house and how Tane would do some small projects when he was next in town.

"Do you have time for one more thing?" Emily asked, and Tane grimaced, looking at his watch.

"Sorry, Mum. If we don't get going soon, we will be late to the tour. And I don't think we'll have time to check into our hotel now."

She pouted, but led us to the door, kissing Tane's cheeks and then mine. "Come back and visit soon," she called as she waved goodbye. "You too, Claire!"

We both breathed a deep sigh once we pulled away. Mine was knowing that the fake date part was over. Now that we were leaving Auckland behind, I didn't have to fake being Tane's girlfriend anymore.

I wondered what Tane's sigh was for. Was he glad to be away from his mom? It had been a full-on weekend, and I was tired.

But not too tired for the Talk.

I ripped it off like a Band-Aid.

"Why did you stop our kiss last night?"

Tane's forehead wrinkled, and he glanced over at me to read my face. I tried to look genuinely curious and not overly horny.

"I guess I thought we should take it slow?" His voice pitched up at the end, unsure.

"I'm leaving in a couple months, Tane. And I'm horny."

He tried to hide his pleased grin, ducking his head and looking out the window. "I didn't want to just assume you'd be okay with a quick bang."

I snorted at *quick bang.* "I'm not okay with a quick bang. A quick bang sounds rushed and unfulfilling. How about a happy medium of a full night in a hotel room, like one near Hobbiton?" I arched an eyebrow playfully and Tane laughed at me.

"You're pretty straightforward."

"Maybe it's because of the situation with Devon, but I like to be straightforward about these things. And if a guy can't talk openly about sex, then he's not worth sleeping with. I like sex. It's worth the effort."

"I agree," he said, smile still in place.

"Also, I didn't sleep well last night because I couldn't get off and that's all your fault."

Tane, to his credit, didn't seem too perturbed by my confession, but he looked thoughtful, driving with both hands casually on the steering wheel.

"You couldn't get off last night?"

I rolled my eyes. "Of course that's what you focus on."

He shot me a look. "We'll get to the rest. Why couldn't you get off last night?"

"Excuse me, sir, did *you* get off last night?"

"Yes."

Annnnnddd now my brain was stuttering over Tane jerking himself off.

"Claire." He snapped a finger, and I refocused my eyes.

"I didn't get off last night because I didn't bring any toys with me here. I can't get off on my fingers, unfortunately." I rolled my eyes. "Bodies are complicated."

"How do you get off?" Tane asked.

"I feel like we're getting distracted."

He smirked. "Fine, but we'll circle back to that. I promise I won't leave you unsatisfied again."

Yes, please and thank you. "That's a good promise." I grinned at him.

His smile slowly drooped, though. "And you don't want to date me. Got it. So you're looking for, like, friends with benefits? Or just the one night?"

I thought back to two days prior, Tane calling himself a "fat fucker who drinks too much" while mourning the loss of his rugby career.

"I would totally date you," I said. "Honest as the day is long, I would date you. But there're a lot of reasons not to."

He took a deep breath in and out. "Right, like the fact that I'm technically your boss and you're leaving soon."

"Eh . . ." I said, shrugging. "I think it's a bit late for that concern."

He grinned and this one hung on a bit longer. Until it started to smolder. "That means that tonight . . ."

A flutter of anticipation settled in my belly. "Tonight you're promising me orgasms."

"And now you have to tell me how you like to get off so I can fulfill said promise."

Tane's eyes were on the road, but I could feel his full, undivided attention. "It's actually pretty easy with a partner. Penetration usually works."

The grin Tane gave me now was full of promise. Weight settled down low in my body and I squeezed my thighs together.

Tane shifted in his seat. "Penetration. Hmmm." His gaze turned inward and I could practically see the porno in his brain.

I got lost in my own thoughts too until my phone dinged.

I looked down and read the text from Iris and smiled.

Iris: No. I might have a stack of photos somewhere. Just say the word and I'll go Martha Stewart on that shit and make you a photo album.

Me: So old-school.

Iris: I'll even use glitter.

Me: Maybe we can do it together when I get back to the US.

"Who are you always texting?" Tane tipped his chin at my phone.

"My sister, Iris. She lives in Chicago with her boyfriend."

"You two close?"

I sighed and leaned back in my seat, putting my phone down. "We talk a lot, but rarely see each other. I miss her."

I told Tane about her job in Chicago and her boyfriend and how supportive she'd been of me. "She's actually the bubbly customer-service one. I love bartending, but sometimes my personality gets in the way.”

“Like with me?” Tane shot me a side glance.

“Ha. Yes. Foot in mouth with that.”

He shifted and changed lanes on the highway. “You love bartending, but you don’t drink alcohol much.”

It wasn’t a question, but I knew what he meant. “Nah, most of the time I don’t like the feeling of being drunk. Especially because I’ve seen bad things happen when people are drunk. Or even questionable things. As a bartender, I always worry when customers get drunk. Do they know that person they’re leaving with? Are they safe?”

“What is it about bartending, then, that you do like?”

I studied the countryside, thinking. “It’s a bit like Goldilocks.”

Tane snorted and I grinned again. "Bear with me here. Some drinks are all alcohol, super strong and burn your throat. Some drinks are all syrupy sweet and you can't taste the alcohol." I paused for a minute. "You sure you want to talk about this?"

"It's fine," he said quickly, "but thanks."

"Okay, well, the good drinks, you can taste the alcohol, but it complements the flavors. It's not just masking the booze. It's complex and creative. A good mixed drink is really good."

Tane nodded, looking thoughtful. "You do seem to have a way with it. You've done a great job."

"Thank you." I beamed.

"And I know you won't like this. But I'm going to put it out just once and then I'll never do it again." He looked at me, a teasing sparkle in his eye. "I think you're hot as shit. Your legs, the nose stud, your hands. They do it for me."

"My hands?" I held them up in front of my face. "I think you can compliment my hands all you want."

"I like how they feel in mine."

All right, *that* made my cheeks nice and rosy and gave me warm flutters.

"And I do think you're hot, for the record. You're big and thick. Have you seen your ass in your little rugby shorts? It's like a big, juicy peach." I bit my lip, trying to picture it underneath his clothes.

That earned me another snort.

"How far up does that thigh tattoo go anyway?" I peered over into his lap like I'd be able to see it.

"You'll find out tonight, it sounds like." He grinned and I squeezed my thighs together again. The tension was getting thick and I needed to channel it somewhere else before I self-combusted.

"You've got the grumpy thing going on. Your sister's right—you scowl. It's hot." The corner of Tane's mouth flickered up. "On top of that, I did have a really good time this weekend. Your family is fun, and I loved watching you with them. And you're a good dancer. And, hey! You had a great sober weekend, right?" I smacked his arm with the back of my hand. "That's something you should be really proud of."

"Aw, ya know. My family's supportive. No one pushed me or nothin'."

"Don't downplay it." I poked him in the side. He jerked away and captured my finger before I could poke again.

"I'm *driving*," he said, but he was laughing.

I turned the conversation back to the important topic. "We're attracted to each other, but dating isn't going to work out. Let's just have some fun, okay?"

"Okay." Tane's grin turned mischievous. "So, my ass, hey?"

FIFTEEN

"Have you been here before?" I asked Tane as we settled into seats on the tour bus. We were at the offices of Hobbiton, where our group had gathered for the Evening Banquet Tour. Our cars would be left behind in the parking lot as we ventured to Hobbiton, the real-life movie set where they filmed some scenes from the Shire.

"No, I haven't."

"You have seen the movies, though, right?"

Tane rolled his eyes. "Of course, Claire. Who hasn't?"

"Okay, just making sure. You don't seem that excited."

Putting his elbow on the armrest between us, he watched me, eyes dipping to my lower lip, which I nibbled on in excitement.

"I don't know," he said. "I watched the movies, but I never read the books or thought much about them." He leaned in a little bit closer. "Why do you like them so much?"

I thought back to entire days spent playing Dungeons & Dragons and how the Lord of the Rings franchise had inspired characters and quests. Not the main ones, of course—no one named their chaotic good elf Legolas—but others. "I think the movies were a framework to build on with me and my friends. That's one of the ways we expanded our creativity when we played D&D." I shrugged. "It was influential. It helped give us better visuals that we could relate to."

Tane nodded beside me. We were quiet for a moment, watching people filter onto the bus, and then Tane leaned toward me again.

"I may not be really excited for your nerd fest"— he nudged me playfully and his voice dropped lower—"but I am *really* excited for afterward."

A flush crawled up my neck as the bus pulled away and a welcome video started playing on the mini-screens above us, introducing the movies and giving us the history of the Shire. I watched with interest until Tane elbowed me and pointed out the window.

And there it was. The Shire. We unloaded from the bus, our tour guide walking us around and explaining everything we saw, answering questions, but mostly I just took it all in.

The hills rolled vibrant green, interrupted by the colorful hobbit doors and flowers lining the fences and paths. Little details, like Easter eggs, were sprinkled throughout: a "no admittance except on party business" sign hanging from Bilbo's gate, birds' nests and clothing lines and wishing wells.

Wonder rose over me, that this would be tucked away in New Zealand, a fictional world come to life right here for anyone to visit.

Some of the hobbit homes were smaller than others, something to do with scale and filming human actors. Tane posed for me, stooping low to get through one of the doors, placing his giant hand on the tiny doorknob, and I doubled over with laughter.

The best part of our tour was that it was late in the day. We were the only group there, and the lighting was soft and warm over the Shire. Paper lanterns switched on, an orange glow reflected in the still pond, while the Party Tree stood sentinel.

It was picturesque and perfect.

Our tour ended at the Green Dragon Inn, where we'd be served dinner. The warm wood gleamed, lit by the fireplaces and torches on the wall. I grabbed a beer for myself and water for Tane and returned to the corner where he was waiting, holding the table for us.

We sipped our drinks and watched out the window as the string lights switched on outside, the daylight disappearing.

"Is it everything you hoped it would be?" Tane asked me.

"More," I said. "It feels real. Like there should be hobbits and magic in the world. I love it." I turned back to the bar. "It reminds me of Haft & Hops a little bit."

"Really? How so?"

"It's the atmosphere, I guess. It's warm and cozy and familiar. Wood and warm light."

Tane hummed in agreement. "It feels romantic."

I tilted my head and tried to muffle a smile. "If it were a date—if—it would be a pretty good one."

Humor laced his voice. "Too bad it's not a date."

We paused, watching the bar and the people around us. Most of the rest of the group was made up of tourists. Not many Kiwi accents that I could pick out.

"Just for the sake of discussion: How is this different from a date?"

"There's no hope of a relationship, Tane," I pointed out.

"But," he said, gearing up to argue, "it's a romantic setting. I'm buying you dinner. We're going back to the same hotel where, unless I muck it up big-time somehow, we're having sex. Guaranteed orgasms, right? I think you'd agree most dates don't include that."

"Too true," I conceded.

"But at the same time, most dates don't have a guaranteed relationship at the end either."

Damn it. He was kind of making sense.

"What's in it for you? Why do you want to call this a date so badly?"

He shrugged. "Maybe an ego boost? I haven't had a date in years." He gave me a self-deprecating smile.

"Years?" I raised an eyebrow.

"Not since I retired."

"Hang on a minute. You're hot, rich, and you played professional rugby. How are you not every Kiwi woman's wet dream?"

He shrugged and frowned down at the glass in front of him, playing with the condensation on the outside. "While I was on the team, I definitely pulled my fair share of women." His tone was flat, factual. "Once I wasn't a pro anymore, I felt like I lost my luster. Or maybe it was my behavior for a while after my forced retirement. Either way, it's been a while."

"But that time I saw you in Wellington, when I was moving hostels? You were meeting a woman for dinner then."

"Ah." He shifted a little bit, embarrassment rolling over his face. "She wasn't a date. She's a sobriety coach."

"What about . . ." I scrunched up my face, trying to remember the name of the woman he'd been pictured with at some black-tie rugby event. "Blond? Busty?"

"Nelly?"

I nodded and something dark flashed across his face. Anger, or hurt?

"We were nothing." He said it curtly enough that I felt the sting. "She was a gold digger, basically."

"Her loss. Well, if it makes you feel better, it's been a while for me too. I'm sure I haven't forgotten anything, though." I winked while taking a sip.

"I may have forgotten things, but I take instructions well." His mood shifted, eyes twinkling at me in the firelight. "So tell me: If your fingers don't do it, what does?"

"Ooo, looking for tips?" I teased him, leaning in close so as to not be overheard by the guests around us. Tane came closer, and I brushed my lips against his ear while I answered, my voice dropping low. "I like to be bent in half and fucked hard."

Any response Tane had was lost as we were interrupted by the announcement for dinner. I stepped ahead of him, assuming he'd follow.

The guests were led to the next room over, where long family-style tables were set up and laden with large platters of food. Everyone took random seats, and I turned around to ask Tane where he wanted to sit but found that he wasn't behind me.

I backtracked to the main room. Tane was still standing behind the high table like a loner at a high school prom.

Come on, I gestured.

Tane looked pointedly down at his lap, which I couldn't see in the shadows under the table. I twisted my lips to keep in a laugh.

I snagged a seat next to a couple who introduced themselves—Amy and David from America—and put a napkin on the back of the empty seat next to me for Tane. A staff member drew our attention and described the dishes. As he was explaining dessert—something called pavlova—the chair next to me pulled back and Tane took a seat. He mock glared at me and I gave him wide innocent eyes.

A steady hum of conversation grew as plates were passed and stories shared.

And Tane was back to his fake-boyfriend setting. He had his arm around my chair, giving gentle nudges while he teased me, making eye contact when someone asked us questions as if we were a couple.

"Where do you live?" David asked.

"*We* live in Wellington," Tane answered.

Later: "How did we meet?" the British couple across the table asked.

"*We* met at his bar."

"Are you Tane Taumata?" This at a whisper from a server crouching down between our chairs.

And once, during a lull in the conversation, Tane leaned toward me: "I can't stop thinking about it."

Our fingers were entwined under the table and Tane brought my hand discreetly to his lap to feel the thick erection behind his zipper. It shot a chill up my spine.

This time, it felt less fake. We weren't doing it to trick anyone. We'd never see these people again. These touches, these quick kisses, were just for us. Just for anticipation.

There may not have been dwarves or elves, but it was still pretty magical.

SIXTEEN

"Hi, we're checking in. We have a reservation for two rooms under Taumata, but we're only going to need one," Tane said to the receptionist at our hotel. It was late, and we both may have eaten too much food. The pavlova, a favorite dessert in New Zealand, was light and fluffy with meringue and fruit, but I ate three servings of it and the sugar rush crash was hitting me hard.

"Certainly." The receptionist smiled at Tane, batting her eyelashes. "I thought that might be you checking in. My dad's a huge fan."

She's a huge fan.

I was standing next to Tane, but my duffle bag was slung over my shoulder between us. For the first time tonight, someone wasn't assuming we were a couple. Even though Tane had *just* said we'd be sharing a room.

"Tell him thanks for the support." Tane smiled politely and then stifled a yawn behind his hand.

"Would you like some coffee?" the receptionist offered, gesturing to a machine to the side of the lobby. "I'm happy to make you one, and I'd love to hear what you've been doing since you retired."

Tane winced. "Just the room, thanks."

"No worries, let's see here. Are you sure you don't want to keep the second room?" She typed into her computer. "Oh wait, your reservation only has one room. And it's a king-sized bed. Too bad we're all full up." She pouted.

Tane and I looked at each other and burst out laughing.

"Okay, wait, Nina definitely said I'd have my own room."

Tane pinched the bridge of his nose. "She said you'd have your own room for the wedding."

"But I assumed . . ." I trailed off, realizing Nina had done this on purpose. "Oh, she's good," I whispered, narrowing my eyes at Tane.

"She made her own loophole," he agreed.

The receptionist passed two key cards over the counter and eyed us. We composed ourselves and moved over to the elevator to go up to our room. When the door closed, I turned to Tane.

"You should text Nina. Tell her there's only one room at the hotel so you're making me sleep in the truck."

Tane shook his head, shoulders shaking in laughter again. "My sister. God, she's such a busybody."

"It almost kills me to admit that she's getting her way here," I said. "She didn't need to short us a room; we would have been sharing one anyway."

"I'm not telling her that."

"You could tell her that you gave me the room and shacked up with the receptionist instead."

Tane swiped his face with his hand. "I had literally just told you I haven't dated in forever and then I immediately got hit on."

"She just proved my point," I said as the elevator opened into the hallway. "She thinks you're a hottie too."

I stopped in front of our hotel room door, the first one on the right. Instead of pulling out the card and unlocking the door, Tane stepped closer to me, crowding me into the doorframe, an echo of the night before. "She doesn't push my buttons like you do," he said, voice low and eyes hooded.

"I can push buttons," I agreed, whispering the words against his lips as they brushed over mine.

Tane's mouth slanted and I opened to him, allowing his tongue in on a gasp. I let my bag drop to the floor as his big arms came around me, pressing me into his body and lifting me up to his level. Tane's kisses were perfect, just the right amount of tongue for us to tangle, but backing off in time for me to get ragged inhales when I needed them. He nipped my lip, then dropped his hands down to my ass and gave a good squeeze, hiking me up around his waist.

"Let's get inside," he said, pulling back to fumble with the key card. "And then you can show me how to push your buttons."

I laughed as the door opened and I clung to him while he kicked our bags inside the door. He grunted when I nibbled his lip a little harder and we tumbled down onto the bed, Tane catching himself on his palms while I flopped off him.

We toed off our shoes, crawling up to the headboard, and I tugged the hotel comforter down underneath me and kicked it farther off the bed. Tane let it fall to the floor.

"So you don't like using hands," he said between kisses, letting his fingers graze up the inside of my shirt.

"I do like hands," I amended. "They just don't get me off."

Tane tugged me up to sitting, straddling him, so he could pull my T-shirt off. He paused, his eyes roaming my skin. The majority of my tattoos could be covered by shirts; the half sleeve on my right arm peeked out from under short sleeves and, of course, there was the icosahedron on the back of my neck. But the half sleeve grew roots on my chest—literally. Vines and roots in a woodblock print twined out from my arm onto my chest and back.

I followed Tane's gaze down to my first tattoo, a tribal band that curved over my ribs. I had gotten it at seventeen, thinking it was so cool. It wasn't long before I was cringing looking at it. It hadn't been good to start, and it hadn't aged well. But now, after having seen Tane's—and everyone else's—intricate and detailed tattoos, I really wished I didn't have it.

I stretched to the side, looking down at the dark blocks that stood out against my pale skin. "It's a shitty tattoo, isn't it?" I tried to laugh, but my attempt fell flat.

"It's simple," Tane said diplomatically. "But I like seeing it on your skin." He ran a thumb along the outline, trailing up from my side to just below my breast, and I shivered. That thumb then skimmed between my breasts, over the thin strip of material of my bra in the middle and up to where one of the vines dipped onto my breastbone.

Then he brought his head down, kissing that same spot and trailing the tip of his tongue up the vine. On either side of his body, my thighs squeezed.

"Do you like being eaten?" he asked, his hot breath skating over my shoulder.

"Oh fuck" was the only answer I gave, and he pushed back onto his knees between my legs while he unbuttoned my jeans and hooked them and my underwear together and tugged them off. A rough hand wrapped around my ankle and pulled me down the bed. I looked up just in time to see Tane's mouth open, his tongue flat and applied directly between my legs.

I bucked my hips off the bed, but Tane pinned me with one of his beefy arms and devoted himself to licking and sucking me. Minutes later I tensed up, my mouth opening in a silent gasp as I came on his tongue.

I closed my eyes as Tane disappeared. A condom wrapper crinkled, and when I opened my eyes again, he was back. "Legs up now?" he asked.

"We might need a towel," I said, eying his sheathed cock. It fit his body nicely, a little curve and a thick head. "And a little warm-up first."

Tane disappeared into the bathroom, returning with a towel that he folded up and slid under my hips. Then he was on his knees, guiding himself toward me. I spread my legs farther, opening up for his hips and thighs.

There was pressure and give, and then he was inside me. He was slow and careful, watching my face and gently rocking until my ass was nestled into the cradle of his hips. Then he looked down, dark eyes wide and hot.

I looked down too, following the trail of tattoos and flesh to where we met. Tane pulled completely out and back in. Then again. I felt my wetness spreading, each thrust getting slicker than the last.

"Okay, now you can put my legs up."

He gave me a wicked grin and shifted back, hooking his arms under my legs. I shifted too, settling my ankles onto his shoulders. His hands came to my hip bones, gripping me and giving him leverage.

"Like this?"

"Yeah," I said, nodding.

He leaned forward, making eye contact. "You told me you wanted it hard. 'Bent in half and fucked hard' you said."

I nodded, my breath coming out in a whisper, the anticipation so high and tight inside me.

Without warning, Tane pulled out and slammed back in. The pleasure made my eyes lose focus and I cried out when he did it again and again and again. He leaned into me, stretching my legs and hitting me deeper. "Oh God, right there," I babbled.

Two strokes later I came, my eyelids, my knees, my thighs, my *ovaries* clenching together. Tane stilled and, despite not being able to see him, I felt his attention, the press of his lips on my calf.

Tane's voice was quiet. "You okay?"

I nodded. "Legs down. Please."

He obliged and I took a deep breath, filling my lungs and feeling just how sticky and wet I was.

"Twice," Tane said, his voice holding a hint of wonderment. "Eighteen-year-old me is very impressed."

I laughed and stretched my arms over my head, popping my back and rolling my shoulders. I reached out to Tane and used my gimme-hands. "Come here."

Tane leaned down so I could wrap my arms around his neck, pressing his chest to mine and carefully stretching his legs out. I hooked my calves around his thighs and pressed my lips to his. A rumble went from his chest to mine and he rocked into me.

We kept it up like that, slow and gentle, Tane being careful not to crush me. Our tongues tangled and I felt every grunt, every little thrust, and then each pulse as Tane came.

SEVENTEEN

The next morning I awoke to Tane shifting on the bed beside me. He'd been a heavy weight next to me all night, and I often woke up to the feeling that gravity was conspiring with Tane to suck me into cuddling with him.

I didn't mind.

"Morning," I said. I lifted my head and looked around. The hotel curtains were doing a good job of blocking the light. The clock was over on Tane's side and I couldn't see it without making more effort.

I flopped my head back and closed my eyes. Tane moved around, bouncing me slightly on the mattress.

"How do you feel?" His voice was thick and sleepy.

I scissored my legs, feeling the good kind of soreness—no pinches or sharp pain, just the dull ache of muscles stretched and tender. "I feel good." I cracked one eye open. "You?"

He was facedown on the bed, his cheek smashed into the pillow, lips loose and floppy. "I'm good too."

A smile broke out on my face. "I feel a bit bad," I said, and Tane quirked an eyebrow at me. "We only get one night, and we did my favorite position. Not yours."

After Tane's grand finale last night, we had both cleaned up and passed right out. My limbs were still heavy, my mouth cotton-filled and my brain groggy. I'd slept hard—a busy weekend of social pressures, touristing, and killer orgasms would do that to a girl.

"What is your favorite position?"

Tane grinned at me slyly. "Well, there's no need for me to tell you, right? We won't be doing that again. Back to work tomorrow, hey?"

I pouted at him. "I bet I can guess. If I guess right, will you tell me?"

"No." Tane raised himself up onto his elbows to look at the clock. "Shit," he said with a laugh.

I lifted my head, and on seeing the clock, I asked, "What time is checkout?"

Tane reached for the bedside phone. "Fifteen minutes ago."

"Fuck."

———

"Doggy style," I said. We were in the truck, empty travel mugs between us and the caffeine counteracting the sex coma.

Tane snorted in surprise. "What?"

"I'm trying to guess your favorite position. You said you'd tell me if I guessed it."

"I never agreed to that," he argued.

"So it's not doggy style?" I gave him side-eye.

He sighed. "No."

I pursed my lips, thinking. "Please tell me it's not missionary."

"It's not, but what do you have against missionary?"

"It's boring."

"It's romantic," he countered.

"Are there any wild and crazy Kiwi sex positions?"

He sputtered at that. *"What?"*

"You know," I explained. "Like Canada has the Snowpile or the Full Mountie."

Tane screwed up his face. "We don't have sex positions like that."

"Are you sure? I feel like I should search for this." I pulled out my phone and ignored a message from Iris. I dictated as I typed. "New Zealand. Sex. Positions."

The search results were a wasteland, so we played a game making up sex positions for Kiwis.

"The Manuka Mindbender," Tane said.

"Okay, that's where you dribble honey over my —ahem—honeypot"—he groaned at my bad joke—"and lick it off with tongue swirls."

We came up with three more before we drove past Lake Taupo, which was one of the places Nina had recommended I visit. The lake itself was beautiful, even though I only caught a glimpse of it here and there from the road.

But the real attraction was the volcanic activity. There were hot springs and sulfuric bubbling mud and geysers.

"I wish we could stop for a visit," I said wistfully.

"You've got a lot of the country to see," he said. "You sure you can't afford a car?"

"Not yet, but speaking of which, thanks for driving."

He shrugged my words off. "Easy as. I like driving. So 'not yet,'" he said, circling back after my dodge. "Don't take this the wrong way, but your pay is pretty good. And I've seen the hostel you're staying in. Is there trouble back home?"

"No, it's just . . . I borrowed money from my sister to come here. And I do need to pay her back. Her boyfriend makes good money and they live together, but they still have separate finances. I kind of get the idea that he's a dick about it too. They had a fight soon after she lent me the money. She didn't say that's why they fought, but I think that's probably it."

"Do you like him?"

"I don't know him that well," I replied honestly. "When she moved to Chicago and I was still living in Boston, she usually called from her lunch break at the office. I didn't interact with him anymore. Now she calls when she's on her way home from work, if I'm not working a lunch shift. Or when she's getting ready for work and I'm just getting off work."

He nodded.

"What about you? Do you like Nina's husband?" I asked.

At the question, Tane grinned. "I do. He's quiet as, which I'm sure you've noticed. But he's a great dad and has always had Nina's back. I know her hours are tough; being a mum and working at a bar means she doesn't see the kids often."

He was quiet for a moment, tapping his finger on the wheel and frowning slightly. "I need to take more responsibility around the bar. Get her home more often."

I reached over and squeezed his forearm. "I'm sure she'd like that."

The rest of the drive passed with easy conversation and stories and when we pulled up to my hostel hours later, I was disappointed that the weekend was over.

Tane let the truck idle at the curb as he pulled my bag out of the back.

"Froggy style?"

He grinned. "Nope."

I frowned. "I'm running out of positions I know. I hate giving up." I stuck out my bottom lip for effect, but he wasn't swayed.

He looked up at the hostel. "So this is it, huh? Our one-night stand is over and done."

Right. That. I took a step back. "I didn't want to know what your favorite position was anyway."

He took a step forward, ignoring the space I had put between us. "Probably for the best. If you'd guessed right, we might have actually had to do it. Compare notes, you know," he teased me.

"How horrible," I deadpanned.

His smile was easy and affectionate, and I marveled at how we had grown on each other. It had nothing to do with the sex, of course.

"Claire," he said. "Thank you for coming with me this weekend. You made it more fun." He bit his lip. "Seeing my family and a little bit more of my country—even if it was incredibly dorky— through your eyes was a breath of fresh air."

I flushed, pleased. "Well, I enjoyed your family. And your tour guide services."

We both smiled, shuffling a little and, argh, I didn't really want him to say goodbye. But it was for the best.

Right?

Right.

"Bye, Tane. See you tomorrow."

He nodded, hands in his pockets, before leaning forward to dust a kiss across my cheek. "Night, Claire."

EIGHTEEN

Tane was everywhere. Or at least it felt like it. If I was working, he would hang around the bar. He came in with the youth coaches after practices when I was working the lunch shift, he was there giving Nina the afternoon off, and when the bar was quiet, like when I was cleaning up at the end of the night, he was always there.

Sometimes we would order takeout and eat a hot meal at the end of my shift, or he'd be cooking breakfast in the morning when I came in. I started eating most of my meals at the bar.

He was being a sneaky fucker.

We'd both agreed to a one-night thing. And here he was trying to charm my pants off.

I couldn't put my finger on it. He still had a glower around him a lot, but he definitely smiled more often. He wasn't touching me like he had when we were faking a relationship, but the ghost of his hands was on me, the memory of a flirty smile in my mind.

I was imagining all these things that weren't there. If anything, he was avoiding touching me. He still backslapped the guys, hugged Nina, put steadying or supportive hands on the staff. Perfectly acceptable touches, the normal affection I'd grown to expect.

Except for me.

And I found myself wanting to touch him. All. The. Time.

Had our one-night stand fried my brain?

It must have, because I didn't last very long. On Tuesday night the week after the wedding, I leaned across the bar where Tane was sitting and quietly asked him, "Butter churner?"

His gaze snapped up to mine and a spark of recognition flickered in his eyes. "No."

Damn it.

I'd been searching the Web for crazy sex positions, and, let's be honest, fantasizing about them a little bit.

I moved down the bar to close a tab, and a moment later Tane snort-laughed.

"What?" I called down the bar.

He shook his head. "I just looked it up."

The next night, I whipped him up a cranberry-and-rosemary faux-gin spritz, handing it to him and raising my voice so he could hear me over the crowd.

"Spork?"

The corners of his mouth shot up and he shook his head. "Nah."

The next afternoon, when I got off my shift, a black cotton something was folded up over my purse. I shook it out to find that it was a T-shirt with a print of Smaug in vivid orange and yellow. A piece of paper fluttered to the ground. I picked up a Post-it note that read, *Whatever your guess is today, no.*

I chuckled, straightening up until I heard a voice behind me.

"What are you guessing?"

I spun around to find Nina behind me, a bemused look on her face.

"You read it?" I clutched the note to my chest, already defensive for Tane's sake since he wasn't here.

"He asked me to put it in your purse today. It was just folded up and the note slipped out."

She spread her hands wide, a *What can you do?* look on her face.

"I was trying to guess his favorite Lord of the Rings character."

She blinked at me, surprised. "I'm not sure he has one."

I fluttered the paper. "Oh, he does, but I guess he's just not going to tell me until I agree to . . . watch the movies with him."

"He wants to watch the movies with you?" Nina frowned, obviously confused as to why her brother would want to sit through a nine-plus-hour movie marathon with me. "I knew you both had gotten friendly, but I didn't realize you were doing movie nights together."

"We're not," I said, and then firmed up my voice to say it again. "We're not. This is just a stupid game and a thank-you for being his fake date." I held up the shirt.

"Uh-huh," Nina said, not entirely convinced, but she left me alone anyway.

The next day, Tane was the opening manager. I got there a bit early and I found him on the floor of the stockroom, sorting boxes of straws.

The door shut behind me with a click and Tane looked up.

I crossed my arms. "You aren't going to tell me, are you? No matter what I guessed yesterday, your answer would have been no."

Tane rolled to his feet, dusting off his pants. "What were you going to guess yesterday?"

I told him and he shook his head. "I was right. That's not it." Color rose to my cheeks and I was irrationally upset about his confession. "Why are you doing this?"

He studied me carefully. "It's just a game, Claire, a little joke between us. What does it matter?"

"You said, if I guessed right—" I startled myself with the words, and looked at Tane, wide-eyed.

A smile flickered over his lips before he tamped it down. "I said if you guessed right, we might have to try it together." The smile crept back up; he couldn't keep it down and it was smug as hell. "You want to do it again, don't you?"

"Shut up." I swatted at him, blushing furiously. "I do not."

Tane crowded me against the closed door. "You do." His smile was miles wide. "All right, you really want to know what my favorite position is?"

"Yes," I said. Tane looked down at me, close enough that our bodies nearly touched.

"It's bending you in half and fucking you hard," he said, as if it were obvious.

"What? That doesn't count. It's *my* favorite position."

"Well, it was so fucking good with you, it ruined all my other favorite positions."

I half-heartedly pushed against his chest. "Still, you could have picked any—"

My words were cut off by Tane's lips on mine. He hadn't touched me in eleven days and I was *not* counting, it was just that . . .

Ah, fuck it. I definitely wanted Tane again.

His hands were all over me, tugging at my hair, grabbing my ass, and we kissed so hard, we had to break away on a gasp to breathe.

"Fine, I want you. Let's not make a big deal of this, okay?"

He grunted in agreement.

"This isn't serious." Kiss. "The rest of my time here is going to fly by." Kiss. "I might not stay in Wellington." Kiss. "Your sister can't know."

That gave Tane pause. "How are we going to hide it from her?"

"I could sneak up after my shifts."

He pulled back slightly. "She closes every night. I could come to your hostel?"

I winced. "My bed is tiny. I barely fit in it, and if you stay too many nights, I get in trouble with the hostel. I'm only paying for one person."

Something clattered outside the door and I guessed we weren't alone anymore. Tane pressed a kiss to the side of my neck that had me shivering. "We'll figure something out." He pushed off the door and gave me an easy smile. "Let me finish sorting these boxes and we can talk more later."

I left the stockroom, ready to start my day and definitely unprepared to hide the giant smile on my face. But I did my best to tamp it down. Thankfully, Nina was off for the afternoon, so she wasn't around to witness the disappearance of my resting bitch face.

Later, when we had only a few groups out back, Tane sat across from me at the bar as he cashed out one of the servers, a small frown of concentration on his face.

"Why does Nina close every night?" I asked, leaning back against one of the coolers as I wiped off menus.

Tane's lips turned down even farther. "The few times I tried to close back in the day, I drank too much and didn't do it properly. We agreed I wouldn't anymore."

I wiped another menu while Tane counted brightly colored bills. "You're sober now," I pointed out.

"It's about earning her trust back. She needs to know I won't muck it up."

The faith of sisters. That I could understand.

NINETEEN

Okay, intellectually, I knew why you shouldn't sleep with a coworker, or your boss. You could get fired, sexually harassed, etc. Yes, I knew. Bad, bad Claire.

But also . . . it was fucking hot. Now that we had discussed a second night together, Tane came down every time that I worked. If a buddy came in, or a rugby fan, he stood opposite them behind the bar, chatting, or maybe even took a seat next to them. I could see the man Tane used to be when people asked him about his rugby-playing days. His eyes lit up, and the die-hard rugby fans, well, they often kept him going long into the night, and this new Tane, this sober Tane, would offer them autographs as he corralled them out the door at night so we could close.

I wasn't the only one who noticed. Tane without the smell and sway of booze was a hit with the ladies. But when things got too personal, he'd stand up, or stride away, making an excuse to check something for the bar.

And on top of these layers, this new Tane was the man I'd slept with. The man whose fingers had dug into my hips, who'd gripped my body, who'd grunted low and guttural as he'd made me come.

And the reward was a passing touch. A steamy glance across the room. Maybe even an ass grab when we were the last ones doing cleanup, or a hot kiss in the stockroom.

But we hadn't done anything further yet, just teasing each other and sneaking kisses for three weeks. The more I thought about it, the more I realized that him living here made it complicated. Now that I was paying attention, in the mornings when I was opening, if he wasn't downstairs yet, I could hear him clomping around. Even if we were able to slip upstairs undetected, we'd have to bang quietly and somehow manage to get out again.

One Saturday afternoon in March, we had a joint bachelor and bachelorette party out in the range. Most people seemed to be about my age, and definitely the bride and the groom. The bride was from Australia—or "Straya," as I'd heard about fifty times already today, and as I'd gathered from my time here, there was a friendly rivalry between the two countries.

"STRAYA!" the bride shouted upon coming back into the bar from outside. Her friend, a redhead whose skin was flushed from being outside and drinking, rolled her eyes and guided the bachelorette to the bathroom.

When they returned, the redhead asked for water, and I quickly filled two tall glasses and set them down in front of them.

"Thank you," she said. The other woman slumped forward, putting her mouth on the rim of the glass and trying to slurp the water out.

"You're welcome. She's having a good bachelorette party?" I asked.

The redhead cocked her head at me, scanning my features. "You're American?"

"So are you." We grinned at each other.

"Do you know each other?" the bride asked.

We both laughed. "Do you know my cousin in Perth?" the redhead asked.

Her eyes widened. "You have a cousin in Perth?"

"No."

She stuck her tongue out and ducked down, slurping again.

"Where are you from?" the redhead asked me while I slipped a straw into the glass for the bride.

"Boston," I said, letting my accent really pop. "You?"

"Seattle."

"Nice. You live here now?"

She shook her head. "Just passing through. You?"

"Same, kinda. I'm here on a working holiday visa."

"Oh, that's nice. I didn't even know those were a thing until I was too old to do it."

I nodded. "Yeah, it's been good to get out and see the country. There's lots to do and it's not too far."

"Not like Straya," the bride chimed in.

"I'm Mia," the redhead said.

"Claire."

"Lila!" the bride screamed. "Claire. Claire. I have to tell you something." She put her elbow on the counter and leaned toward me.

I grinned at her, amused. "Let me guess, you're getting married."

Lila nodded sagely. "But also, you are *beautiful*."

That familiar cringe hit me, but not as hard as it had in the past. Mia laughed, and I did too. I knew Lila meant well.

"You're beautiful too, Lila. And unfortunately for me, you're taken."

She looked down glumly. "And I'm straight."

"Doesn't mean you can't have a crush on me." I winked at Mia.

"She's taken too," Lila said. "We're going to be . . . sister-wives?"

Mia put her face in her hands. "Lila, no."

"What are we going to be?"

"Sisters-in-law. But not really."

"Why not really?" Lila frowned. I busied myself with wiping down the counter. This was none of my business. "You love him. You *kiss* him. You want to *marry* him." Her lips tipped up and she danced a little bit on her barstool. "I bet you'd even have his babies. Your babies would be so cute."

"Let's try a sailing season together first. We have a boat for a baby."

Lila snorted.

"Where are your menfolk?" I asked, saving Mia from her drunken possible-future-sister-in-law. Lila wobbled on her stool.

"Out throwing axes, probably."

Tane passed by, and instead of pushing my hips against the sink in front of me, I might have swayed back just a little bit. Our clothes brushed against each other's, and I turned my head slightly to try to catch a whiff. Tane always smelled so good, and I thought he'd been out axe throwing earlier.

But what really made my stomach flip was that way Tane slid a hand over my hip, giving me a squeeze. In another time, the bar empty, I pictured Tane using that grip to tug me backward into his body.

I watched him open the door to the storeroom, and as he turned to grab the knob and close it, our eyes met.

Fuck, he was so hot.

"Who was *that*?" came a breathy voice. I turned my attention back to the two women at the bar. Lila stared at the stockroom door, while Mia just looked amused.

"My boss."

"He's beautiful too. What do they put in the water here?"

I laughed, then leaned in to whisper, "He's kind of a jerk." I peeked back at the closed door and dropped my voice even lower. "A hot jerk." A hot jerk who was probably waiting for me right on the other side of that door.

And then I felt a bit bad about it. Could I call Tane a hot jerk anymore? He had been a jerk; alcohol changes people. Instead of an asshole, Tane had turned out to be sweet and kind. And okay, yes, grumpy as fuck sometimes.

Lila nodded, bringing my thoughts back. "Hot jerks can be good for some things."

"Who is a hot jerk?" Two men had walked up behind my customers. The one who spoke, the shorter and stockier of the two, threw his arms out just in time to catch Lila as she squealed and threw herself at him.

"Eivind!" she exclaimed.

He smirked down at her, bemused. "Hello, lil Lila. How are you feeling?"

"We're getting married this weekend." She leaned into his arms and he tweaked her nose.

With the guests distracted, I slipped aside and made eye contact with Alec. "I'm going to grab another Tanqueray," I told him, and opened the door to the stockroom.

"You just can't help yourself, can you?" Tane's voice teased me from the dark when the door shut behind me. The lights were off, with just a sliver of bright light under the doorway casting a very faint glow.

"Me? You're the creeper hanging out in the dark waiting for me." A soft chuckle, and hands glided up onto my hips. Tane's lips were soft and warm, but I pulled back before we could get too deep. There were a lot of customers here and I couldn't do that to Alec.

"You know," Tane said into the dark, "I enjoy teasing and kissing you more than I think I've ever enjoyed even sex with anyone else."

I couldn't decide if I hated that it was dark—I wanted to see Tane's face when he said that—or grateful so he wouldn't see my reaction to what may have been the sweetest thing anyone had ever said to me. "Dangerous words, sir."

Tane was quiet, and then I really did wish the lights were on. What was he thinking? What was he waiting for?

"Do they scare you, *ma'am*?"

The word sounded funny in his accent, but it didn't detract from his meaning. This was getting serious, at least to him.

I cleared my throat. "I really do need to get a bottle of gin. That's what I told Alec I was doing."

"Ready for the lights?"

"Yeah." I blinked when they turned on, Tane's hand beside my shoulder on the switch. He looked at me carefully.

"You okay?" he asked, earnest.

"I told you this wasn't serious." Even to my own ears, I sounded petulant.

Thankfully, Tane was just amused. "Who said it was serious, Claire?" He leaned down, nose to nose with me. "You can't tell me how I feel. If I want you to know how I feel, I'll tell you. And I won't know how you feel unless you say it. Don't worry, your feelings are safe." He pressed a gentle kiss to my lips. "Protect yourself all you need, Claire; you know where to find me."

He turned his back to me, scanning the shelves. "Which gin do you need?" I told him and he pulled down the bright green bottle and passed it to me.

"I look forward to getting you alone again soon. I'll remind you how much fun it can be." With that, he winked and was gone.

TWENTY

"We should get away soon," Tane suggested the next week, a Thursday evening after the crowds had started to die out and we finally had time to breathe. We hadn't spent time together aside from a few stolen kisses in the stockroom, and one particularly heavy make-out session behind the storage shed in the yard.

"Where do you want to go?" I asked him. We were alone behind the bar, polishing glasses.

"What's still on your list?" he countered.

A customer raised two fingers and I poured him another beer, thinking back on my New Zealand bucket list. When I returned to Tane, I'd decided.

"Glowworms."

"Ah, good choice." He paused, thinking. "You like camping?"

"Maybe? I dunno, never done it before."

"There's a lake up by Tauranga that has glowworms. It's nice—less crowded than some of the other spots. We can rent kayaks and paddle to see them. And it's autumn, so the temperature is not too bad. I'm keen if you are?"

Over the weekend, we pieced together our plans. Tane was going to pick me up Monday, and I assured him I would find camping gear for us since he was driving. I half-heartedly tried to suggest flying when I found out it was a six-hour drive, but Tane would have none of it.

"I *like* driving," he'd said.

Just like our drive to Auckland, Tane picked me up early. Perhaps, because we knew each other better, he was more relaxed, more energetic. He whistled as he drove and pointed out the sights, even as I tried to sleep in the passenger seat.

For lunch, we stopped for meat pies and coffee at a small kitschy bakery. I ate a pork belly pie while Tane finished off three of various flavors before we started back on the road. I was more awake, and asked Tane questions about his time traveling for the New Zealand rugby team. He was lecturing me on the rules of offsides as we pulled into a parking lot next to a large lake. There were a few pop-up trailers and tents set up on the shamrock-green lawn, people milling around barbecues or picnic tables.

Tane checked his phone. "Plenty of time before dark. Let's get set up."

We converged at the back of his truck—excuse me, ute—and Tane lowered the gate.

"Where did you get the gear anyway?" he asked me, grabbing bundles of stuff from the bed and walking it out onto the grass.

"I asked at the hostel, and one of the managers made some calls for me. This German couple had been driving around with camping gear, but they're staying at the hostel for a week to be close to downtown."

Tane crouched, his finger tracing over the label on the biggest bundle. "I'm not sure this tent is going to be big enough."

"It's for two people," I pointed out. "See?"

"Did you by any chance mention to them that the second person is, well, me?"

"I haven't told anybody," I said quickly. He frowned at that. "I'm sure it'll be fine. How small can it be?"

He pulled the drawstring, opening the bag and spilling the contents out onto the lawn. "Let's see what we've got, eh."

———

Our tent was tiny. Tane couldn't even fit in it lying down; he had to curl up on his side, which he was currently demonstrating while I peered in from the flap.

He grinned from the ground. "You have to snuggle with me."

"It's not my fault you're giant. Seriously, were you *bred* to play rugby?"

"You're pretty tall yourself, ma'am. Come on down here." Before I could protest, Tane had tugged my hand off my knee and sent me tumbling down beside him.

"Oof. Brute." I pinched his side, but he turned me away from him and tucked me against his side. Tane made an excellent big spoon, his chin tucked above my head and his bicep under my cheek.

"You fit me so nicely," he commented, reading my mind.

I shifted my hips, trying to find a comfortable spot on the ground. "There's an air mattress, you know."

He tugged me closer. "Just a minute. It's been a while since I've held you."

We lay quietly, listening to the noises of the bugs and breeze around us. A car door closed, someone coughed. The temperature was cool, but the sun was bright and quickly warmed the tent up. Tane's breathing was deep and even.

"Are you asleep?" I whispered.

"Yeah, nah," he said in a drowsy manner that did not at all convince me.

"Tane." I poked him. "Come on, let's finish getting set up and then you can nap."

He grunted and rolled off. We finished setting up the tent and Tane did get a nap in. I set off on a trail instead, just a short little path full of ferns and moss in damp, humid air. When I returned, we had an hour to go before sunset and my stomach rumbled. When I made enough noise, Tane roused and pushed me toward a picnic table. He pulled out an honest-to-God wicker picnic basket.

"Where did you get that from?"

"Borrowed it from Nina."

Inside were all kinds of dips and snacks, a smorgasbord of food to get us through the night and morning.

We weren't the only ones unpacking food. Our neighbors were a family of five, the kids old enough to run around mostly unsupervised. The father had shyly asked Tane for an autograph, and then politely let us be. While we ate, one of the kids fed crackers to a black swan, something I wasn't even sure I had known existed before seeing it with my own eyes.

"Do you want kids?" Tane asked me out of the blue.

I choked on my pita chip. "Wh-what?"

He gestured at the little boy. "You're watching the kid. I just wondered."

"I was watching the swan. Its eyes are *red*."

"So is that a no?"

"God, Tane, I don't know. I'm twenty-five. I don't have to make those decisions yet."

He shrugged, then went back to eating his food.

"Do you?"

"Yes," he said, with more firmness than I'd expected. "I like my cousins, the young ones. And I'm getting older, you know."

I nodded, not really knowing. "How old are you?"

"Thirty-two."

"Positively ancient," I deadpanned. I turned my attention back to my food, attempting to feign disinterest. "What about serious girlfriends? Ever had any?"

Tane stared out at the lake while he chewed and swallowed. "Not really. The rugby schedule was tough to keep up with. Lots of arm candy, hookups. And then after my injury . . ." He waved his hand over the table as if casting dice. "You know, I wasn't pleasant to be around."

He wiped the crumbs from his hands and washed down his last bite with a gulp of water. "I guess no one's ever appealed that much to me. No one's ever been life-changing."

Life-changing. Devon had been life-changing, but not in a good way.

"Come on," Tane said, rising from the table. "Let's get the kayak set up so we can be ready to go when it gets dark."

It did take us time to drag the kayak out to the launch, strap ourselves into life vests, and check our headlamps.

We paused on the shore to watch the sun disappear without much fanfare—it was a cloudless day, and the sky, devoid of a textured canvas, slipped steadily into darkness.

Not long after, we settled into the kayak, and I sat in front of Tane. It was the kind of two-person kayak where you sit on top of the molded plastic. Tane's legs didn't quite fit into the footholds, so his big feet went up on either side of my waist.

I belatedly realized we should have done this sooner. I had no experience paddling a kayak before. Tane tried to coach me from behind, but our paddles clicked and clacked together more often than not.

"Claire," Tane said, sounding amused. "Just let me do it."

I let my paddle rest on the rim of the kayak as Tane quietly stroked behind me. I had layers on, but wet spots from the paddles were making me chilly and the temperature was dropping.

He knew where we were going, and as it got really dark out, we followed our headlamps into a small inlet. The shore crowded us on either side, trees touching over our heads, blocking out the night sky. In the patches of my headlamp, I illuminated mossy rocks dripping with condensation. It was otherworldly, Jurassic, even.

We slowed, gently bumping against a large rock on my right. When I glanced over, the edges of the light caught Tane's hand, his big paw gripping the moss, and . . . not really holding us in place, as the water was calm, but it felt stabilizing.

I reached out and touched the rock myself, poking the moss and giggling when it gave under my fingertips.

One of the spots of light went crazy, bouncing around the vegetation as Tane took off his headlamp. The kayak shifted as he leaned forward, breath whispering into my ear. "Ready?"

My hand went to my headlamp and found the button to turn it off. "Ready."

"Three . . . two . . . one." We clicked our headlamps off together and I held my breath as we were blanketed in darkness. I blinked, but nothing changed. It was all just black. I sagged a little, disappointed.

"Why aren't they . . ."

Tane cut me off with a nudge on my shoulder.

"Look to the left," he said, mouth still pressed tightly against my ear.

I did. I blinked a few more times, my eyes still adjusting to the dim lighting. Was it . . . was that . . . ?

Ohhh . . .

They slowly came to life—whether they'd been lit up the whole time or not, I wasn't sure—and Tane and I were surrounded by neon-green pinpricks of light. Where they clustered together, there was enough light to cast a glow over the rocks and moss.

It looked alien. It looked like something out of *Avatar*, a microscopic city that quivered and glowed. It looked like the Milky Way, tucked into this little corner of the world, swirling only for us.

There was a light splash as Tane's feet slipped into the water and his grip around my waist became firmer, hauling me backward toward his chest. I leaned into him, resting my palms on his forearms over my front.

And like that, we drifted.

TWENTY-ONE

There were bathroom blocks in the camping area, and by the time we got back, we had them all to ourselves. I showered quickly, dressing in yoga pants and a T-shirt and hustling back to the tent. Tane was already there, curled up on his side.

I put my things in the truck and tried not to slam the door. The other tents and campers were dark and the night was quiet.

Tane's face was right inside the screen door of the tent, and when I shone my headlamp in, he squinted. The zipper was loud, and the air mattress let out a plasticky fart noise when I crawled in.

Despite the chill, Tane was shirtless in his sleeping bag, the bare tops of his shoulders peeking out at me over the edge of the zipped-up bag.

"Hey," I whispered. "Can't we, like, zip the bags together or something?"

I could barely see the corners of his mouth curve up in a smile. "You want to snuggle, Claire?" he teased.

"I want *something*." I trailed a finger along his shoulder, and Tane scoffed.

"Oh really?" His voice dropped lower. "Sex in here? There're kids next door."

"We can be quiet." I leaned forward, pressing a kiss to his neck while my finger tugged the edge of the sleeping bag down a bit farther, looking for one of his broad dark nipples.

Tane shifted rhythmically, humping the air, and plastic flatulence emitted from underneath him.

"Okay, okay," I said, laughing. "No sex."

"Yeah, nah. No sex. But come here anyway." Tane tugged me down onto my side, wedging our legs between each other and wrapping an arm around me.

I rested my head on the pillow—the air mattress had a long bump at the top that pretended to qualify as a pillow—and was nose to nose with Tane.

He pressed his lips to mine gently, affectionately. We kissed, slow, lazy kisses, hardly moving anything but our lips and tongues.

"I've missed kissing you."

"I've missed kissing you too. I have a love-hate relationship with you living above the bar."

Tane grinned against my mouth. "Yeah?"

"I get to see you almost every shift. That's good. But I wish we could sneak up to your place sometime."

He nibbled my bottom lip.

"Have you thought about asking Nina if you can close sometime? If you and I are the last ones there . . ."

With a sigh, Tane rolled over to his back and we both ignored the mattress noises. "When the bar first opened, I had no interest in really running it. Nina insisted that if I was going to help her with money, then I had to be part owner, too. At the time, that just meant that I could come and go as I pleased, drink my nights away, and I was fine with that."

"But now," I said, "you're behind the bar instead. Do you think she doesn't want you to take on more responsibility?"

The shadow of his head turned toward me. "She's still scared. She doesn't trust me yet. It's only been a few months, so I can still see the worry in her eyes. I don't want to ask yet, because she'll say yes, and then sit at home worrying that after everyone's gone, I won't be able to control myself. She'll find me munted on the bar floor the next morning."

"I think she has more faith in you than you know," I murmured. But I didn't push it. It might not be Nina who Tane worried about, but himself.

———

I woke up with a start. Something was rustling outside the tent. Something big. The grass whispered under its feet as it snuffled the tent, its nose running along the thin material. It pressed against the fabric, bowing the material in toward my face.

Tane slept like a rock next to me. The tent was filled with the soft gray glow of early morning, and I reached behind me. My open palm explored while I stared at the animal outside.

I felt around. Tane had shifted to face away from me. I found a cheek, and patted. When nothing happened, I fishhooked his mouth and he woke up with a snort.

"Shh . . ." I hushed him.

"Wha . . . Claire?"

"Tane," I hissed. "There's something outside. Do you . . . do you have bears here?"

Tane froze, which I took as a very, very bad sign.

"Did you hang the leftover food up last night?" he asked.

"What? You didn't tell me to!" The thing outside took an extra-large huff and I dropped my voice again. "What do we do?"

"I'm going to get a better look."

Carefully, he turned over, propping himself up on one hand to see around me. The air mattress farted some more, but the animal outside didn't seem to care. Tane's other hand curled around my waist, pressing me back against him. That was reassuring. He was a big dude, right? Surely he could fight it off long enough to get help. "Hm. That's pretty big," he whispered.

"What do you think it is?"

"Well, have you heard of the drop bear? It's an invasive species from Australia." I gripped his forearm. "But I think, in this case—"

"BLEAT!" erupted right in front of my face. I gasped, and Tane started to vibrate behind me, laughter bubbling up. "BLEAT!" the sheep said more insistently.

"You fucker!"

At my explosion, the sheep took off, little hoofbeats sounding against the grass. Tane's laughter burst out of him, and I uselessly pushed him away from me. Moving him was like trying to move an elephant. I heaved and only succeeded in getting myself stuck in the space between the tent wall and the air mattress.

"Jesus," he said, choking between laughter. "I'm gonna piss myself."

I'd been swallowed by the gap, so I couldn't see Tane's desperate escape from the tent to make a break for the restrooms, but his laughter faded with him.

TWENTY-TWO

After repeatedly assuring me that there were no bears—or any predators bigger than a house cat or stray dog—in New Zealand, we drove away from our campsite in the morning and made our way into Tauranga. We visited the beach, hiked up the nearby Mount Maunganui, and watched paragliders take off from the top.

We were back at the campsite with fresh supplies in time to watch the sunset and have another picnic dinner.

The next day we packed up our too-small tent and the rest of the gear into the back of the truck. I climbed into the cab, but before I could buckle my seat belt, Tane put a hand on my thigh.

"I had a lot of fun with you," he said, squeezing my leg.

I grinned over at him and leaned across the console. "I did too."

Tane met me in the middle, pressing his lips against mine. When we backed away, I bit my lip, longing for more, remembering the way we had kissed in the tent, the slow, quiet slip of Tane's lips over mine.

When I looked up at his eyes, Tane was staring at my lips. He let out a grunt, bringing a hand up to cup my neck and pull me back in. We met harder this time, our mouths opening in a kiss slicker and more urgent than I'd ever had before.

Maybe it was the pent-up energy, or maybe it was how Tane had seemed unbothered by the sexual tension I felt. Flickers of heat in his eyes were rare; he was usually so controlled. But now he groaned and pressed harder. I tilted, opening as much as I could as his thumb slid across the front of my throat. I swallowed, and his grip, momentarily, tightened.

And then he was gone. He bent over, turning the key in the ignition and bringing the engine to life.

"Fuckin' kids," he muttered. "Fuckin' tent."

And then he peeled out of the parking spot and toward the road.

I laughed, and as the miles passed under us, Tane relaxed, sliding into a comfortable posture. He let me pick the music, and I hummed along. A few songs in, I tilted my head, watching him. He wasn't listening to the music, and his mind seemed to be elsewhere.

Raising his hips slightly, Tane reached down and adjusted himself in his shorts. A flare of desire shot through me as I caught sight of the bulge. He was hard.

I turned back toward the road ahead of us. We were out in the sticks, miles and miles of pastures on either side. Propping my left foot up on the dash, the farthest one from Tane, I closed my eyes and slipped my hand under my jeans. I kept two fingers together, making small circles on my panties, pressing harder with each go-around.

"Claire," Tane warned. "What are you doing?"

I didn't answer, pressing up with my heel and lifting my hips higher, wriggling down in the seat. The cotton was starting to get damp, my fingers shifting back and forth over my clit. I wouldn't be able to get off like this, but it would serve its purpose—torturing Tane.

The truck slowed and I opened my eyes just in time to brace myself as we turned down a country road. A minute later Tane pulled over and slammed the truck into park.

"Pants off," he commanded.

Both of our seat belts clanged against the windows as we stripped out of our clothes. Tane leaned over me, pressing a button on the side of my seat to electrically move it back. He grunted impatiently as I slowly moved backward, inch by inch. I encouraged more grunts by kissing his neck, just behind his ear. He switched buttons, and I started to recline until the headrest hit our bags in the back seat.

"I'm going to fucking regret this," he said, but he swung a leg over the center anyway and settled between my thighs, kneeling on the floorboards. Two thick fingers plunged into me, pumping hard. "God, you're fucking wet."

He brought his mouth down on mine hard and pulled back, his tongue, his fingers, leaving me momentarily while he slipped the condom from his wallet on.

"Legs up."

I curled my legs and raised my ankles up to his shoulders. Tane pressed down on his dick, nudging into me. He gave a few experimental thrusts, but the angle was wrong. He was too high, and his knees had nowhere to go.

We tried a few more positions, and finally settled on Tane's feet pressing against the front of the footwell, his knee wedged against the door. He couldn't have been comfortable, but he didn't seem to care.

The sound of our bodies slapping together echoed in the cab. Tane bent forward, bracing his hand on the shoulder of the seat over my head. Even though the tips of my toes brushed the ceiling of the car, I was nearly bent in half. Every stroke out hit my body with sharp pleasure.

"Tane, I'm going to make a mess," I warned him.

"Don't care," he bit out between strokes.

"Of course not, it's"—I bit down on my lip with a particularly hard thrust—"my fucking seat."

He reared back, neck bending at an odd angle to give him room to pull off his shirt, and he reached between us to use it as a towel, wedging it under my ass.

"Better," I gasped when he plunged in again.

Sweat trickled down his torso, getting caught here and there in the dusting of hair. I wanted to run my fingers through it, catch up the drops with my tongue, but I was pinned down, my arms uselessly flailing about, trying to grab onto anything I could as Tane pounded harder.

I squeezed my eyes tight, turning my head to the side where Tane's hand was braced.

"Hurry up, Claire." The words were a deep growl, a warning and a threat.

"I'm . . . I'm . . ." The pressure crescendoed and my whole body clenched beneath him. He kept stroking through my orgasm, chanting little things I could barely hear through the roar in my ears. I knew he stilled. I thought he came. But hell if my brain could experience anything outside of my own pleasure.

We cleaned up using the shirt and both relieved ourselves on the side of the road. Not a single car had turned onto the small street, and with tall cypress trees on either side, we were blocked from the view of the highway.

I left my seat where it was and lounged as Tane got us back on our way to Wellington. He hadn't bothered to fish out a different shirt to wear, so he sat bare-chested and hummed along to the music.

TWENTY-THREE

I'd been at work for less than an hour and I was ready for it to be over. It was the day after our trip to the lake. Alec hadn't fully restocked the bar the night before, so Nina and I had to move cases of beer around before the evening rush came in. And every time I bent down, an ache in my lower back grew.

Did I have a UTI? I was always sensitive to them, especially with condom usage, but I'd been pretty good about peeing after sex with Tane.

I dropped a case in front of the reach-in cooler where Nina was crouched down with the door open, and as I stood up, I placed a hand on the small of my back. And that was when I found the lump.

"What the fuck?"

Nina looked up, her quizzical eyes changing to concerned when she saw my grimace and posture. "Oh no. Claire! Were you lifting with your legs?"

I laughed. "Yes, I was being careful. I think there's something wrong with my back. Here," I said, turning around and lifting my shirt up. "Can you see a bump? Right there?" I ran my hand over it again. It felt like a vertebra had popped out of place. Wouldn't that kill me? Or paralyze me? Did I need an X-ray?

Nina's finger, cold and damp from the cooler, touched the knob on my spine. She hummed, then touched it harder. "Does that hurt?"

"No, not really. Do you see anything?"

"There's no bite or sting, but it's swollen, like an insect got you."

"Is it red?"

"No . . ."

I placed my hand on the top of the bar to support my weight while she poked and prodded me. "You know, a medical degree would be really handy right now."

Nina laughed and swatted my backside.

"What's going on here?" Tane's voice boomed, and I looked over my shoulder to see him stepping out of the office.

"Tane, come look at this. Claire's got a bump and some back pain. You've seen physical therapists before. Did any of that soak in?"

Instead of coming around the bar, Tane looked right at me, his eyes wide in a *What the fuck?* look. I gave him a *What the fuck?* look right back. He gaped at Nina, his mouth dropping open and flapping for a moment.

Okay, Tane's gone insane.

"It's almost like you banged your spine, Claire," Nina said. "But you would notice that. Maybe you have a bad bedspring. Or maybe . . . you said you went kayaking this week, right? Maybe paddling the kayak over and over against a bad backrest would do this. Like if you were really paddling hard, banging your back over and over again in the same spot . . ."

And right then it hit me what my swollen spine was from. I flashed back to fucking in the front seat of Tane's truck, my ankles up over his shoulders.

FUUUUCCCKK.

I looked up at Tane, our mutual *What the fuck?* faces morphing into panic. Nina was still droning on and on about banging and, honestly, if Tane weren't so panicked, I'd probably be dying of laughter because I swore she just said "banging sideways."

Tane and I stared at each other as Nina wound down. ". . . but here's the thing: It's probably none of those scenarios. Because the injury is from some crazy sex position you two tried and the looks on your faces right now are great. Claire, ice your damn back and try not to point out injuries you get from banging my brother again. Tane, for fuck's sake, don't break her."

"You knew?" was the only thing Tane could think of to say.

"Of course I knew. I've seen you two play grab-ass on the CCTV anytime you think someone's not looking, and obviously you forgot about the camera we have in the stockroom." She rolled her eyes and waved her hand, walking back to said stockroom to pull out more cases of beer. "Don't bother trying to hide it now."

Tane and I looked at each other as the door slammed shut. I was still leaning against the bar, my shirt up around my ribs, lower back exposed.

He broke eye contact first, stepping next to me. "Does it hurt?" His fingers lightly traced the bump. "Did it hurt when we were in the car?"

His voice was edged with worry, and he rested his big palm on the side of my back, fingers still tickling the spot. I straightened, knocking his hand down. "It didn't hurt when we were doing it, I swear."

A smile flickered across his face.

"Maybe I shouldn't be lifting things." I watched him as the teasing words came out. "Sure could use a big strong man to help restock the bar, though."

It was Tane's turn to snort and roll his eyes. "Fine, I'll help Nina. But now that she knows, you're coming home with me tonight after your shift."

"Whatever," I called out dismissively, hiding my excitement as the door slammed closed behind him. I overturned a crate and placed beers into the cooler.

When the door opened again, Tane and Nina were each carrying boxes—one for Nina, three for Tane. They put the boxes down next to me and before I could say thanks, Tane leaned down and tugged my hair, pulling my head back. He bent over and brushed his lips against mine, sending chills down my body. "Don't whatever me."

I grinned as he pulled away, and the quick kiss in public—in sight of Nina and everything—was branded on my lips like no other kiss before.

TWENTY-FOUR

I had thought it was hot when we'd snuck around in public. Shared looks, stolen touches, all the illicitness of it should have been what made it hot, right?

But instead the whole thing being out in the open made it about a thousand times worse. All through the night, Tane caught my eye. Sometimes he smirked, sometimes he smoldered. Every time, he made my stomach flip.

Where we used to dance around each other, we now touched. Tane stood at the taps, chatting with a customer, and instead of stepping away as I came in for a beer, he lifted an arm up, letting me reach in and pour it. I leaned against him, his hand settled onto my hip. I shifted against him, and he shifted back.

"You all good?" he said to me quietly as I straightened with the beer. His thumb slipped under my belt, tugging me.

It was too busy to have a spare moment in the stockroom, so nothing entirely illicit happened. But I was built up.

When the night started to wind down and it was time to send some of the staff home, Nina asked me if I wanted to go. I glanced up at Tane and he caught my eye, walking over and ducking down to hear Nina better.

"I was asking Claire if she wanted to call it a night."

Tane shook his head as he bowed down toward us. "We'll close up tonight. If that's okay with you, Nina?"

Excitement fluttered in my chest. Not only was I staying the night, but Tane was asking Nina to take a big step with him.

Nina glanced between us. "Yeah?"

Tane held her gaze. "Sure."

She walked off. "I'm out!" she shouted over her shoulder.

Tane chuckled and I looked back at him. "We're closing?"

"We're closing," he confirmed, leaning in, his voice dropping low and breathy. "And then I'm going to get you so fucking loud."

I *shivered*. I shivered there behind the bar, barely able to keep my eyes open. Tane was fucking naughty.

We worked through the rest of the night. Group by group, the customers left, and one by one, the staff went home.

Tane disappeared out back to straighten the furniture and clean while I polished and counted cash while the last of the customers paid their tabs.

"Have a good night," I called to their backs.

A few minutes later Tane came in. "Everyone's gone?"

I nodded.

He stalked to the front door, clicking the lock into place and bolting the top of the door.

I tried to ignore him, finishing my paperwork and leaving some notes for the morning staff. I was off for lunch, but I'd be back in the afternoon.

The warmth of Tane's body hit me first, the soft rustle of fabric as his front touched my back. There was no press of urgency or tangle of fingers and limbs. Just his solid, steady weight, a warm gust of air on the back of my neck.

I shivered again, my hands stilling over my work.

Tane's lips met the back of my neck, right over my icosahedron. A wet open-mouthed kiss, followed by the breeze of the air-conditioning cooling my skin. My pen clattered to the counter.

Another kiss, an inch higher, and Tane's nose buried in my hair with a big, deep inhale.

"I have to finish this," I whispered.

"I'm not stopping you" was his response.

"Yes, *sir*, you are."

He huffed a laugh. "If I really wanted to prevent you from doing your work, I could. This is nothing." His hands appeared on the counter on either side of me. He flattened his palms against the counter, his fingers stretching out. They were so big—proportioned to him, of course, but next to my slender ones, they seemed massive.

"Claire," he said. "Fucking hurry up."

I broke away from him to put the cash in the safe—the most important thing to do before I left—and then came back and did the math for the credit receipts twice, all while Tane's kisses were moving from the back of my neck to the sides. When his tongue flicked out and his teeth caught my earlobe, I bucked against the counter, pushing my hips back and into him. He was hard.

Tane wrapped his arm around me. "Well, now you've fucking done it."

I squeaked as he hoisted me up against his chest, his other arm coming around to pin my arms down. "Tane, I'm not done!"

"Don't care."

Tane lifted me up, my feet coming off the floor, and strode to the door leading upstairs, and I laughed and squirmed. "Put me down."

"Nope."

"*Sir*, I mean it. Put me down right now."

To my surprise he did, and I took my own weight for a moment, my hands on Tane's shoulders as he straightened up and spun me around to face him.

"Thank—"

Tane dipped down, this time hoisting me over his shoulder. "Hey! Sir!" I shouted, swatting his ass.

"Needed a free hand," he grunted, starting up the stairs. I swatted him again and he swatted my ass back.

When he set me down again inside his apartment, I was flushed and laughing. "You brute," I started. "You realize I'm going to have to go downstairs and finish up?"

"Problems for future you," he said, wrapping a hand around the back of my neck and pulling me in for a kiss.

All the evening's tension crested in me so quickly. I felt the answer in Tane, his greedy hands and own barely controlled tension driving me backward. He stepped forward, leading me as his hands met on my chest to unbutton my top. I wrapped my arms around his neck, running nails through his hair and clawing the shirt up his back. I was impatient, scrambling to get skin to skin.

When the last button went, Tane's hand shed the top off my shoulders and we broke apart to get my undershirt and his T-shirt off.

I looked at Tane through half-lidded eyes, his cheeks flushed and eyes vibrant. I loved the swirls of ink on his shoulders, that pop and darkness I could run my hands over.

When my palms ran over his muscles, Tane dropped down to a crouch, working the buttons of my pants and hooking my underwear, dragging it all down my pale thighs. He bent farther, struggling with my shoes and socks, until, finally, I was naked.

I tugged his shoulders, trying to get him up so I could finish stripping us, but Tane pushed me away. My back hit the wall, and in a fluid motion, he rose to his feet, arms hooking under my thighs and lifting me up, spreading me open to him.

"You aren't worried about breaking me?" I teased, gripping the back of his neck. Tane pressed me into the wall, my back digging into the plaster.

"Should I be?" His eyes glinted as he shifted and looked down. I looked too; somehow Tane had gotten the fly of his pants open, his cock hard and bobbing between us. I relaxed my knees, gripping his shoulders and sinking lower as he rolled a condom on and lined us up.

"Ready?" His forehead pressed against mine.

I was mesmerized. Unable to tear my gaze from the sight of us, me slick and waiting, him hard and straining.

Air and the smell of Tane filled my lungs as I took a deep breath. "Ready."

Tane slammed forward, the air sharply leaving my lungs, and I didn't have time to get another breath in before Tane was pulling back and pounding in again.

"Fuck," he said, and dropped a curse in Māori. "That is the fucking hottest thing I've ever seen."

I finally remembered to breathe, and at my big inhale of air he glanced up at me. "You good?"

"Yeah. You can hold me up like this?"

Tane smirked. "You weigh like a quarter of my weight. Light as." His palm squeezed my ass. "Is this angle good?"

He stroked again and I moaned.

"Oh yeah, it is." His attention drifted back down to where we met. "I'm going to make you come like this, up against my wall and fucking loud as."

He started up a steady, reliable stroke, hitting me in just the right place to see stars. Beyond them, Tane stared down at us, his breath coming in hot pants and his cheeks flushing.

With every gasp I gave, he grunted. Tension kept building, and my fingers, threaded through Tane's hair, grew damp.

He stopped and I whimpered. "Claire." Cool air brushed against my face as he pulled back. "Are you okay?" He watched me carefully.

"Yes, very, don't stop."

He laughed, but didn't start up again. "I asked because of your leg."

"What?" I blinked, trying to focus.

"Your leg is shaking."

I looked over and yes, my foot had wandered up by Tane's shoulder and was vibrating.

"Oh, it's good, it's so good, don't stop, I'm almost there. . . ."

Tane chuffed and, *thank God*, got back to stroking. I closed my eyes and tilted my head back. We were both so focused, the sound of our bodies slapping together echoing in the room.

And then my body tipped, the tension popping and snapping as I came hard. Tane gripped me firmly as I cried out, and I might have kicked him in the face.

He stilled, forehead pressed against mine as we breathed together. I assessed the damage—leg still trembling, maybe my fingers, too, lips a little numb, hamstring protesting *hard*.

Lungs protesting too. I gasped out for air and pressed Tane back.

His arms took my weight off the wall, and I grimaced as my legs unfolded.

I closed my eyes and clung to him as he carried me through his apartment to the bathroom. There was a clink and then a swoop and my butt hit the cold, hard toilet seat.

I opened my eyes in time to catch Tane turning on the shower before taking care of the condom. He stood in front of me, hands on hips.

Something niggled the back of my mind. "Did . . . ?"

He tipped his head and I tried again.

"Did you . . . ?"

Bah. Words.

He smirked at me. "Did I fuck you stupid?" he teased, clearly proud of himself.

I snapped my fingers—or tried to—and attempted to put my brain back together after a mind melt.

Tane bent down, running his fingers through my hair and tugging my head back. He gave me a swift kiss and a little tap on my cheek. "Come on, babe, let's get you cleaned up so we can get to bed."

TWENTY-FIVE

It was weird, in a good way, waking up in Tane's bed. First of all, it was giant. And soft. And maybe it felt extra good from the brain-melting sex last night.

I had no idea what time it was, but Tane was next to me, facedown and spread eagle. Okay, maybe the bed wasn't quite big enough.

The shower had brought my body back online, even though Tane had had to help me in and out of it. We had rinsed off and crashed.

Nature called and I used the bathroom, letting out a quiet groan when I felt how sore my legs were. When I came out, I climbed back into Tane's bed and took the opportunity to look around. It was a studio apartment, bare-bones and bachelor. The kitchen had a few dirty dishes on the counter, a small fridge and a stove. A big TV, a massive armchair.

And a big naked man.

I couldn't believe Tane was still sleeping. Maybe he'd exerted himself a little too much last night. Downstairs, soft music sounds and the occasional scrape of a table or chairs drifted up.

I sat up in the bed and focused on the arm nearest me. Tane's brown skin was laced with tattoos, and while I'd seen them before, I'd never gotten to gawk at them so freely. They were all tribal, not a hodgepodge like mine.

He twitched as I traced a finger down his triceps.

"Careful" came his voice, rough and scratchy from the morning. Glancing up, I saw one eye open, watching me.

I slid down, twining my arm with his and pressing a kiss to his shoulder. "Good morning."

His chest vibrated with a chuckle. "Morning. How ya feeling?"

I nipped his skin with my teeth. Even thinking of last night sent a shiver down my spine. "Better."

His grin turned smug, but a phone buzzed somewhere in the room. We both looked up and around, and it buzzed again.

"Where is your phone?" he asked.

"Downstairs, probably. With my stuff."

With a sigh, Tane threw back the sheet and sat on the edge of the bed, scrubbing his face. Another buzz.

"Fine, fine," Tane grumbled, striding naked toward the front door and the pile of clothes nearby. He squatted down, junk dangling in the air, and I giggled.

Before he could find his phone, there was a knock on the door.

"Yeah?" Tane called out, hands finding his underwear instead.

"It's me," Nina said through the door.

I tugged the sheet up to my armpits as Tane covered up his goods. He opened the door, and as small as the place was, I could see Nina at the top of the stairs. She had a hand covering her eyes.

"Are you decent?"

Tane looked at me and I shrugged.

"Kind of?" he said.

Nina scoffed and held her other arm out in Tane's general direction, offering him my bag.

"Claire, your sister called the bar, worried about you. You might wanna call her back." With that, she turned to walk down the stairs and Tane called thanks to her.

He tossed me my bag and I sat up in bed, catching it. "Coffee?"

"Please."

My battery was down to 7 percent, so I wiggled my way over to Tane's side of the bed and plugged my phone into his cord. I had an increasingly panicked set of messages from Iris.

Hi, call off the alarm. I'm fine, I messaged her.

My phone rang with a WhatsApp call immediately.

"Claire!" my sister shouted, exasperated. "My emergency contacts are worthless!"

I rolled my eyes. "They weren't worthless. Nina knew where I was, right?"

My sister scoffed. "She knew you were safe, but she didn't know the important things. Like, if you two were together now, or—"

"You asked Nina if we were together?"

"Babe, Nina and I chatted for an hour. She's a *delight*."

Tane came into my field of view and offered me a mug of steaming black ambrosia. I pulled the phone away from my mouth. "My sister talked to yours for an hour."

"Jesus," Tane muttered as he walked away.

"Well, I'm safe."

"Are you just going to ignore the question? Fine, then did he give you a good dicking last night?" I choked on air. "Did you use protection? I'm not ready to be an aunt, but, man, your babies would be—"

"Okay, okay, Jesus. I don't know. Yes. And yes."

"You don't know if you are in a relationship? Nina knows that you're banging now and he brought you upstairs. That means something, right?"

Tane, in his navy underwear, climbed back into bed with me with his own coffee. I set my mug on my lap and twisted the bottom nervously in the sheets, very aware that Tane could hear everything I said. "I don't . . . We haven't . . . but . . ."

The phone disappeared out of my hands. "Hi, Iris," Tane said to my sister.

"What . . . but . . . no . . . I . . ." I sputtered.

He ignored me. "You're asking questions that are too hard for her this morning."

Iris gushed at him over the phone, her voice high and excited. But then it pitched low and Tane grinned at whatever she was saying. "I hope so."

I squinted at him.

"She is stubborn about that," he said.

Okay, I did *not* like this. I scrunched up my face, but Tane just laughed.

I put my coffee on the bedside table. I crawled *all the way* back across the bed, letting the sheet fall from my body. Next to Tane, I rose to my knees and gently took his mug before straddling his lap and setting it on the other nightstand. Tane's eyes widened.

"Iris, your sister is employing defensive maneuvers. I gotta go."

That was good. I owed Tane an orgasm.

———

Tane insisted that I bring everything I needed for a few nights to his place so I wouldn't have to go back to the hostel at all. Which, of course, meant that almost everything I owned in New Zealand came with me to his place. My hostel room, even though it was nicer than the previous one, was pathetically small, and I wondered if I should give it up. But I was *not* living with Tane. That would just be ridiculous.

But the commute was nice. And Nina let me use her office computer in the mornings to keep up with my job search. A week faded into two and we fell into a routine. When I worked nights, Tane and I did something fun in the morning—usually we'd walk around the waterfront or visit Te Papa again, or, once, I let him treat me to another trip out to Somes Island. Then I'd report for work, and he'd work behind the bar too, sometimes just keeping us from getting swamped on busy nights, other times catching up with his buddies, especially the other youth coaches who had started hanging out at the bar more often.

When I worked the lunch shift, Tane often disappeared into the office with Nina or out back in the range. At night we'd grab takeout for a late dinner and sit out on the deck.

Sometimes Tane was approached for signatures or customers sent him beers, which he gave to me.

But every night ended the same, with us retreating upstairs. If we were early, we were quiet and gentle, kissing and whispering over the noise of the bar below us.

And then there were the nights we closed the bar and had no one downstairs to hear us.

"Excuse me, *sir*, what is going on here?"

I lay on my stomach, head propped up on my hands at the foot of the bed as I watched Tane get dressed. It was the weekend and his youth team had a tournament across town. I had to work later, so I was not in a hurry to get out of bed early.

"What *is* going on?" Tane asked, looking down at himself.

"Come here," I said, gesturing him forward. I gave a tiny tug on the hem of his shorts and they fell to the floor. I laughed as he pulled them back up. "You need to retie those drawstrings. You're losing weight."

"Yeah?" he said, pleased.

I pushed off the bed to my knees and wrapped my arms around his neck. "You look good. The training you do with the youth team"—I'd seen him running alongside the boys—"and not drinking anymore—it looks good on you."

He leaned in and kissed me. "Nina says I look happier too. She blames you."

"Credit where credit's due." I tried to deepen the kiss, but Tane pulled back.

"Babe, I gotta get going." He patted my side, running a soothing thumb over my ribs. "Gonna grab something to eat on the way. Won't have time if you keep distracting me, though."

"Fine," I said, mock exasperated, and pushed off him to flop onto the bed. Tane puttered around, finishing getting dressed and drinking his coffee.

My phone buzzed and I rolled over to its home on the nightstand and checked the screen. There was an email with the subject "Application for Bartender."

I sat up, quickly opening the email and scanning the message.

"Hey," I said excitedly. "I got an interview!"

Tane smiled as he picked up his keys. "That's great. Where?"

I gave him the name of the restaurant and he frowned. "Never heard of that one."

"It's . . ." I scrolled down to the bottom of the email. "It's in Auckland." I glanced up at him, some of the excitement draining out of me. The expression on Tane's face told me he was going through the same thing.

He smiled again, more tentative. "Congratulations. When do they want to talk to you?"

I squinted at the email. "Today. This afternoon."

He nodded and bent over the bed, knuckles on the sheet, and kissed me. "I gotta go. Good luck today, yeah?"

"Yeah," I said half-heartedly. When the door shut behind him, I flopped back down on the bed. "This is why this was a bad idea, Claire," I lectured myself. "Your time is running out."

TWENTY-SIX

I emailed back confirming the interview—no harm in talking to the hiring manager, right? After twenty minutes and several dramatic flops and rolls in the bed, I made myself get up and go downstairs. Nina was already there, based on the clattering of pans in the kitchen. I followed the noise. And my nose.

Nina turned when the doors swung open. "Oh good, you're up. Tane told me to feed you."

I was in charge of toast and juice; the veggies, sausages, and eggs were already cooking.

When Tane didn't have a game day and I was working the lunch shift, we usually came downstairs to cook a proper breakfast, since I wouldn't likely have time to eat until after the lunch rush.

I sat on the stainless-steel counter, feeding bread into the toaster and munching on a piece. I swallowed as Nina dished out breakfast onto plates. "I've got an interview today."

"Tane told me that, too. What's the place like?"

"Upscale. Fancy. Full-service restaurant on"—I checked the map—"Queen Street."

While I'd applied to tons of restaurants and bars in Wellington, I had only applied to places in Auckland that were the dream—jobs that might be a stretch for me with my background, but they offered the kind of drinks I wanted to make, the craft cocktails I'd brought to Haft & Hops.

But I hadn't heard back from many places in Wellington yet. I'd scheduled an interview with one, but when Tane heard where it was, he told me: "Absolutely not." I hadn't been aware that there were places in Wellington where he'd be uncomfortable with me taking the bus or walking.

"Queen Street is great. Lots of traffic. When's the interview?"

I told her and Nina said she'd make sure to give me free time to use her computer. We ate our breakfast at the bar, a little bit of tension in the air.

"Have you talked to your sister lately?" Nina asked me.

It made me pause. While we didn't have a strict schedule, Iris and I usually messaged back and forth most days. But as I speared a bit of sausage with my fork, I realized I hadn't heard from her in a while. Two days? Three?

"I need to talk to her today. I'll give her a report on the interview when it's over." I popped the sausage into my mouth but pulled out my phone to message Iris.

Got an interview today! Wish me luck.

Staff started to filter in and I washed our dishes before reporting to bar duty. Since it was a Friday, the lunch crowd kept me busy. When not running around and slinging drinks, I prepped for the evening shift, mindful that I'd be taking a break for the interview, making sure the ingredients for the cocktails were stocked up and even premaking some mixers.

At quarter to four, Nina took over and I stepped into the office, shutting the door. I turned on the video camera, testing the view and audio, checking my teeth and settling my nerves. A few clicks later, Joe, the hiring manager for McGraves', appeared on my screen. We said pleasantries and he dug into the questions.

"Tell me about what you've been doing at Haft & Hops."

I perked up. This was going to be good for me. The McGraves' cocktail menu was seasonal and local, just like I'd tried to bring in here at

Haft & Hops. I waxed for a bit about discovering the local produce and experimenting with new flavors.

"That's great," he said a little absently. "We've got a pretty solid seasonal menu. You won't be doing menu creation with us."

"Yeah, that's fine. I enjoy it, though. Actually, I also crafted some cocktails based on nonalcoholic spirits. There's an importer that works with—"

"We've got a mocktail menu too," he said.

I bit my tongue. They did, but it was mostly lemonades and juice spritzers, nothing that actually tasted like alcohol.

He plunged ahead, asking about my potential schedule and my visa. "How soon could you get here?"

"Ah well, my six months at Haft & Hops is almost up."

"Well, if you can get here to start Wednesday, the job is yours."

Wednesday, as in five days. I'd have to quit here early, pack up my meager things, fly or take the bus to Auckland—still no car—and find a place to stay. I knew it would come quickly, but I hadn't expected it to be that fast.

Joe interrupted my thoughts. "I'll send you the paperwork. Let me know tomorrow."

"Yes, okay. Thank you." He gave me a distracted smile before signing off.

Right. So. Joe wasn't great. But I wouldn't be working directly with him. I clicked around the McGraves' website again, just to remind myself that the menu was awesome and I had a job offer. A job offer that would keep me in the country for another six months.

My phone buzzed and I pulled it from my pocket, the notification showing up on my phone: an email with the details. Opening it up, I saw the offer and the hourly wage—the higher pay rate made my eyebrows skyrocket until I remembered it was in New Zealand dollars. But after calculating the conversion rate, my eyebrows stayed up. The pay rate for a bartender in Auckland was better than I was making here and much, much better than I'd be getting in Boston.

I checked my other notifications and saw a return message from Iris that had come in two hours ago.

Call me when it's done and lmk how it went!

That was optimistic. I did the math—I was getting better at it—and calculated that it was nearly ten p.m. for her. I was sure she was in bed already.

I got the job! Call me when you wake up.

I put Nina's computer to sleep and stood up, tucking the chair under the desk. My phone, back in my pants pocket, vibrated consistently for an incoming call.

Iris's face looked up at me from the lock screen as I answered the call.

"Hey. What are you still doing up?"

"I've had a busy day," Iris said, sounding tired. "Don't worry about it, though. Tell me about your new job."

"Well, I haven't accepted it yet." I told her about the position, the restaurant, and the pay. She made all the correct noises, but I could tell she wasn't really into it.

"Remind me again why you can't stay in Wellington? At Haft & Hops?"

"Well, I could stay in Wellington," I clarified, "but I would need to find a job here, and so far, no luck. I can't stay at Haft & Hops because my visa only allows six months in one job. Apparently, that's where the New Zealand government draws the line between long-term and temp work."

"You really can't find a job in Wellington?"

I sighed. "Not one that I like, or that Tane likes. He's been a little bit pickier than I have." The corner of my smile tipped up, remembering Tane telling me that I was damn good at my job and needed a place that deserved me.

"I think you should say fuck the job and travel," Iris announced.

"That takes money, babe. I'm still working to pay you back."

"I'll send you the money again. We'll just ping-pong thousands of dollars back and forth between our accounts and the bank will think I've got some odd thing going with money laundering in New Zealand."

As nice as it was, I knew that wouldn't work. She knew it too.

"Want to tell me about your day?" I asked.

She gave a deep sigh. "Chris and I had a fight. I don't want you to worry about it, though."

My eyebrows drew together. "What did you fight about?"

Her hesitation deepened my concern. I didn't know Chris all that well. They'd dated for six months before moving to Chicago, but I was kind of wrapped up in my own shit at the time. I was glad for Iris when she'd moved with him. Of course we cried and promised to visit each other. But I hadn't been able to do that.

"He didn't, like, cheat on you, did he? I'll gladly borrow that money again to fly back and kick his ass."

That made her laugh and I relaxed a smidge. "No, no, nothing like that. We're just having a disagreement about something."

Iris's evasion made me nervous. "Iris . . ."

"Claire . . ." she mimicked back, in the annoying way only a little sister can.

"Fine. Don't tell me."

"Fine, I won't. Go back to work. I'm going to bed."

"Fine," I grumbled, just to be a little bitchy.

"I love you. A lot. It'll be fine, trust me."

I softened a bit, and reminded myself that I certainly didn't know what it took to make a healthy relationship last. "Love you too, Iris."

We said goodbye and I slipped my phone back into my pocket, feeling an anxiousness I couldn't pin down.

———

When I left the office and returned to the bar, the first person I spotted was Tane.

"How'd the interview go?"

"Good. How did your game go?"

"Good." We stared at each other across the bar. When I'd stepped out the door, I'd been thinking of my little sister and not the problem right in front of me: I had to tell Tane about this job offer and we had to have a real, serious discussion.

Suddenly I didn't feel so good.

"I got the job offer."

Tane flinched. His regular grumpy face melted down into uber grumpy. "It's a good one, isn't it?"

"Yeah." I sighed. "Probably the best one I'll get."

Tane swore. "Hey, Nina. Do you need Claire, or is she off?"

Nina looked up from the end of the bar where she was talking to one of the bus staff. "She's off. Go home and quit glaring around my bar."

He didn't even argue about it being his bar too, just spun off the stool and stomped upstairs, leaving the door open.

I grabbed my things and waved goodbye to Nina before following him. The apartment door was open, Tane's back to me as he glowered out the window facing the street.

"This isn't my fault," I started, already on the defensive.

"I know." Tane's words weren't angry or bitter. They were sad—tired, even. He turned back to the window and ran his hand through his cropped hair. "This just sucks, you know? I wish we could find you something here, something that would make you happy."

That was nice, not having to feel like this was my fault. And of course Tane would be this way. Too good to be true. I stepped to him and wrapped my arms around his waist.

"Honestly, the job in Auckland doesn't sound perfect. While the restaurant is nice and everything, it's just a bartending job. Granted, it's not serving shitty beer and vodka sevens all day like some of my past jobs. And the hiring manager's a bit . . . . rough."

Tane's hands rubbed up and down my back. "I wish you could stay in Wellington."

"I can't afford to without a job."

He pulled back a little bit and I looked up, resting my chin on his chest.

"You could stay here in my apartment. Right now we're pretty much living together anyway. Without the costs of a hostel, it would buy you time to look for a job."

"I would like to pay you rent."

Tane scoffed. "I don't pay rent. I own the building."

"It wouldn't be fair, Tane, and I would owe you money." I pushed him away a little farther and he let his hands drop to his sides.

"Fair to who? I'm offering, Claire."

"It wouldn't be fair to Iris," I pointed out. "Or to me. I need to pay her back to feel better about my life and my choices."

Tane crossed his arms. "You are stubborn." His resignation was clear, and I relaxed, glad to not have to argue about it.

"So are you."

He gave me a small grin and bent down, his arms wrapping around me, and we settled in, pressed together and warm.

"Can I come visit you in Auckland?"

"You gonna drive all the way? Sleep in my hostel room with me?"

"I'm not hearing a no."

I grinned up at him. "No, you aren't."

Tane bent his head, pressing his lips to mine. And that night we started saying our goodbye-for-now.

TWENTY-SEVEN

Nina and I worked together to cover my shifts after I gave my official notice. She had assured me that it was fine for me to leave earlier than expected. "With Tane working the bar more," she'd said, "and the slow season, we needed to cut staff anyway." I had made sure to write down all my recipes and even create a few more for the bar to have as backups.

I worked the Saturday night shift, and Sunday morning Tane and I looked at hostels in Auckland. "I didn't realize how lucky I'd gotten here in Wellington," I commented. "These places are not cheap."

In fact, the difference in my pay rate was probably going to go into my hostel. And after my experience in Wellington, I knew that I couldn't handle skimping on a place to live.

Together, we picked a place in a decent part of town that was walkable to McGraves' and had a good rating on Hostelworld.

"Okay, one more thing done," I said after making the booking. "Just have to pack."

"About that," Tane said, getting up from his couch and walking back to his closet. He pulled something out of it, and I heard a *clack-clack-clack* as wheels rolled across the floor. "Even if it's just for the one trip, you needed a bigger suitcase last time I checked."

"Aw," I said, snickering. "One that actually fits all my stuff. How reasonable."

"Well," Tane amended, "it might fit all your stuff. I don't know how much you have back at your hostel, but you need to pack up here first. You've got a lot of stuff in my place."

We both worked through the apartment, throwing things into the new suitcase and putting dirty clothes into Tane's washing machine. When his space was de-Claired, we went downstairs and joined Nina in the kitchen, where she was cooking breakfast.

"Claire," she wailed. "Your last day!" She wrapped me up in a huge hug while Tane prevented the eggs from overcooking.

I spent the day at the bar—not as staff, but as a customer. My fellow staff members said goodbye, and even some regular customers—like Evans and his wife—made sure to come in and have a cocktail to say goodbye too. In fact, Nina encouraged me to indulge in some of my own drinks, and by the time Tane tried to herd me upstairs, I was a little drunk, a little nostalgic, and a lot sad.

"Wait, wait, wait, Tane," I said—slurred—while Tane helped me up the stairs to his place so I could get my stuff. "I didn't do something."

He smiled down at me, bemused. "What didn't you do?"

"I didn't"—I looked around dramatically—"I didn't hit a bull's-eye. Like, how can I leave without doing that?"

He tipped his head back and laughed, halfway up the stairs. "Well, it's not happening today, babe. You're liable to hurt yourself or someone else in this state."

"Well then, what's the point of having both axes and booze?" I grumbled.

Tane continued our journey up the stairs. "You're supposed to be delightfully buzzed when picking up the axe, not on the turps."

"On the turps? I've *never* been on the turps. How dare you. I'm good and properly munted."

He snorted. "Now you're just showing off your Kiwi slang."

We made it up the stairs and Tane poured me onto his bed. He pressed both hands into the mattress on either side of my face. "You can throw an axe again when you come back to visit." He bent in for a kiss. "But you're going to have to practice a lot more if you want to get the bull's-eye."

"Good thing I'm sleeping with someone who owns a . . . a range." The crinkled skin around Tane's smile was like a magnet to my fingers and I poked his cheek. "Sober me won't tell you this, but drunk me wants you to buy me a plane ticket for that visit."

We'd already talked about visiting each other. My schedule at McGraves' would be irregular because they were open every day. It made a lot more sense for Tane to come visit me because Haft & Hops was closed on Mondays, and he and Nina had a regular schedule. He had two consecutive days off every week, whereas I had random days off.

And if I did get two days in a row off, I didn't want to spend them on a slow, twelve-hour-each-way bus trip. Either that or I'd spend twice as much on a flight, which countered my struggle to save money.

"I'm supposed to fold my laundry," I said, halfway to sleep in Tane's bed.

"I'll fold it for you and pack it in the suitcase."

"You just want to touch my black thongs again," I mumbled into the covers, and passed out.

Tane woke me up an indeterminable amount of time later, and wrapped my hands around a mug of coffee. I was still humming with a buzz, but when I hit the bottom of the coffee, it had faded to a manageable tipsy.

"Let me drive you back to your hostel," he said.

Tane carried my bag down the stairs and through the main room, which was significantly quieter. It must have been after the evening rush now, the back windows revealing the deck, illuminated by the floodlights.

I had already hugged Nina about thirty billion times that day, but she came around for one more anyway. Tane drove me to my hostel, where I gave him a thorough goodbye and finished packing. Six hours later, me, my headache, and my new rolling suitcase were on our way to Auckland.

———

Two weeks later I was settling into my new job and Auckland. As expected, the "big city" was noisier and more crowded than Wellington.

As much as I didn't like some aspects of it, I realized this was a really great learning experience for me. I was working with sommeliers and world-class mixologists, and regularly heard the banging and cursing from a celebrity chef coming from the kitchen.

Tane was due to come up in a few weeks to visit. I had a Tuesday off and an evening shift the following day, so I could spend a majority of the visit with him.

My new hostel was nice, but much more expensive than Wellington. I was becoming informed enough about New Zealand politics to understand that property values were a big issue here. *Not unlike Boston*, I thought.

Tane and I talked all the time. It was weird to have what was, essentially, a long-distance boyfriend. Part of me worried that Tane would think of this as a trial run for when my visa ran out.

Part of me worried I would think that way too.

"My drinks done yet?" Kira, one of the servers, asked.

It was possibly the first words that had been directed at me in twenty minutes. It was a busy Wednesday night, and the bar was packed. Standing room only.

At Haft & Hops, I'd chatted directly with the customers. Sure, when it was busy, I'd gotten my to-do list via the ticket machines that printed out orders, but most of the time I worked with the customers. Here, I was low woman on the totem pole. The machine spitith the drink orders, and the servers taketh them away. Over and over again.

"Right here, Kira," I said, putting the last Matakana bottle on the tray. Another order spit out of the machine and I dug right back into the fray. I had to duck and weave through the team of bartenders who were fulfilling drink orders—usually the more complex stuff, too—for the suited men and women at the bar.

One thing I was really happy about, though, was the tips. I had honestly forgotten about tipping. It was not common in New Zealand, but I guess in the busiest area of Auckland, we got enough Americans for there to be tips. I understood: it felt like you were a shitty person when you didn't leave a tip behind, as ingrained as it was in my American heart. It was pocket change to most, but every little bit helped me.

But I had sent a thousand dollars to Iris. I might actually pay her back by the time I left New Zealand.

———

While I talked to Tane every day, he had given me no clue that his mom was going to stop by. My surprise—and pleasure—at seeing her was genuine when she stopped in mid-afternoon and took a seat at the bar with four other women.

"Emily! It's good to see you." I came around the bar to give her a hug, which she returned, and it made my heart pang with how much it reminded me of Nina.

"Aw, thank you, hun," Emily said when she pulled back. "These are my girlfriends: Nina— yes, this is the woman my daughter is named after—Julie, Kiri, and Shivani. This is Tane's girlfriend, Claire."

I flushed at the introduction, but didn't argue. Going around to the back side of the bar, I asked, "What can I get you ladies to drink?"

"I don't suppose you could make us one of your own cocktails?"

I winced. "Not one of the ones that I served at Haft & Hops," I said regretfully.

"Darn it, I knew I should have come down to visit sooner."

I pulled out one of the McGraves' cocktail menus. "Why don't you tell me what kind of drinks you like, and I'll help you pick your new favorite?"

The ladies had wisely chosen to come in mid-afternoon, before the after-work crowd, and once I got them sorted out with drinks, I made excuses to stay nearby and listen to their chatter.

These women had even more funny stories of Tane, like how he snuck out one night as a teenager to meet up with a girl—Tane had started young!—and got caught sneaking back in when his dad thought he was breaking and entering.

The bar got busier, and I wasn't able to pay them as much attention as I wanted. But when they got ready to leave, Emily made sure to kiss my cheek and tell me to come visit anytime.

TWENTY-EIGHT

Another week passed, and the bar was busy every night. I didn't think I'd ever worked in a place that was this busy all the time. Even lunches were packed, with faces starting to get familiar.

Until one of those faces froze me in place.

Devon.

Devon was here, in Auckland, in my bar.

"Hey, new girl, move it" came from behind me.

Devon's eyes caught mine and he smiled and I swear to God, everything tilted for a moment. The world was not right.

One of the other bartenders gripped my upper arms and bodily moved me out of his way.

Devon was still smiling. That patient little smile I remembered too well. The *Ah, she's not quite on the same page as I am yet, but she'll get there* smile.

I told my feet to move. I took a step back, and then another and the rest came easier. Thankfully, I didn't have to leave the employee area to get out of view. The bar led directly to the kitchen, and in the clanging of pots and pans and the hiss of steam and fire, I ducked and ran.

Somehow I ended up in a storage room. Thank God, I hadn't blindly run out back; I'm sure one of these doors would have led to the rear alleyway if I wanted to, but I'd bet good money

Devon would already be trying to find me that way.

I pressed my back against the wall and took huge, heaving breaths. Devon was here. Thousands of miles away from home and a restraining order and he was still here.

What could I do? I literally had no one here. Should I call the police? Would they even be able to do anything?

I had to do something. So I pulled my phone out and called the one person I knew who could calm me down.

"Hey, babe," Tane said, "I thought you weren't getting off till late tonight?"

I pressed the back of my hand to my forehead, telling myself to get the words out.

"Claire? Is this a butt dial?"

"Devon's here," I blurted.

Tane's tone changed instantly. "Where are you?"

"I'm at work. I'm . . . in one of the storage rooms."

I heard a door close through the phone, and the noises around Tane quieted. I could picture him in the office, mean face on and calculating.

"What time is your shift over?" he asked me.

"Eleven." Three hours away.

"Can you talk to your boss?"

I hated the way my voice quavered. "She's usually out on the floor on nights like this."

"Okay, babe. Devon's probably not going to make a scene with the bar being crowded and loud, right?"

"Right." There were a lot of people here. It would be hard for him to interact with me, never mind get me alone.

"Okay, hang up the phone, do your job, and try not to worry about him. I'm going to make some calls."

"Who are you going to call?"

"I've got friends in Auckland. Let me see what I can do."

I guessed that "friends" meant rugby players. The image of having my own behemoth rugby player to escort me back to my hostel made me feel a whole lot better.

I tried not to think about what would happen if Devon followed us.

"Okay," I whispered into the phone. "I can do this."

"You can do this, babe. I won't let him hurt you, I promise."

We agreed for Tane to message me updates, and I'd sneak away to check in with him every hour.

When I got back to the bar, it was a mess.

"Hey, what the fuck is this?" Niko, another bartender, gestured at the ribbon of orders coming out of the ticket machine. "You can't just disappear."

"I know, I know, I'll catch up."

He huffed and walked away. I worked as quickly as possible, but nobody was helping me. My hands were shaking, and I dropped a lemon slice, then a glass, which shattered. The servers impatiently popped in and out, distracting me.

And all the while I could feel Devon down the bar. I didn't look—I didn't want to, but I knew.

After I fumbled another drink, Erin, the manager that night, told me to go home. There were still tickets well past due, and I was useless.

Instead of leaving, I grabbed my things and went back to the storage room. I'd checked in with Tane forty-five minutes ago, so I dropped him another text.

My manager's sending me home. I fucked up too many drinks. I'm sitting in the goddamn storage room again.

My anger overflowed. I *hated* that I was here in this stupid storage room, hiding. I *hated* that Devon was here. I *hated* that I'd left Wellington when I hadn't really wanted to.

I kicked the wall and let out a primal scream. Why did it have to be like this?

My phone buzzed in my hand and I checked the screen. *I'll be at McGraves' in thirty minutes. Don't go anywhere.*

Holy shit. Was this what love felt like? This intense relief, this gratitude that washed over me, that came straight from my heart. The fact that I had *someone* who was willing to ride to my rescue, even though I was an absolute mess, prickled my eyes.

I sat down on an empty keg and burst into tears. I had a really good cry, the kind I needed to get out before Tane got here: sniffling and honking, and thank God I had tissues in my purse.

As I tried to calm down, my tears subsided, and the fight-or-flight response dulled, my brain got to working. How did Devon know I was here? It niggled in my mind a little bit. I hadn't posted anything on social media, and I hadn't been in touch with anyone back home except . . . Iris.

I pulled up Iris's name on my phone and hit call, pretty sure she was asleep.

"Hey, Claire, everything okay?" She sounded groggy.

"Devon's here."

Iris's sharp inhale cut through me, and my Spidey-Sense flared.

"You were the only person who knew where I was." I tried to keep my voice low and even. She wouldn't do this. She wouldn't. "How did Devon find out?"

There was a rustle on the line like she was moving around, and then her breath blew right into the phone a few times until I heard the click of a door.

"He came by the apartment one weekend. . . ."

Oh. My. God.

"How could you?" I fumed, kicking a keg this time. It clanged against the ones next to it, and the empty kegs reverberated.

"Claire, I—"

I hung up the phone, seeing red. It was so much easier to be angry with Iris than angry with Devon. I really wanted to be angry with Devon, not scared or freezing up, but truly angry. But my body wouldn't let me. Instead I could focus on Iris.

My phone buzzed in my hand, a call from her, and I hit ignore. It buzzed again, and instead of just ignoring it, I powered down my phone. Tane knew where I was. He'd find me.

I paced the room while waiting, chewing on my fingernail. Devon had known to come here, not to Wellington, so he must have stopped by my sister's recently. Maybe she hadn't told him. Maybe she'd made some offhand comment that had given him a clue. Or maybe he'd found some clue online. What if I'd been photographed with Tane somewhere? People were always asking him for pictures or autographs. I'd never really thought about the possibility of me being in the background. But how would Devon have even known where to start to look? Who in America even follows New Zealand rugby?

The door opened and I spun, panicked that my thoughts had conjured up Devon. But it was Tane, and behind him was Erin.

"She's fine." Erin breathed a sigh of relief.

Tane stepped into the room and turned around. "Go away," he said before slamming the door.

Two steps and I leaped at him. Thank God, Tane caught me and wrapped me up in his arms. I bawled like a big baby while Tane comforted me.

"I'm sorry," I gasped through my tears. "I don't know what's wrong with me."

He squeezed me tight into his chest and even though I couldn't breathe all that deeply, I didn't care.

"There's nothing wrong with you, Claire." One of his hands stroked the top of my head, soothing me. "It's okay to be scared and angry and a whole bunch of emotions right now."

I hiccupped and pulled back, face-to-face with Tane. "I don't understand why I'm like this, though. How come I can do something like get up in your face and tell you off but I can't do it with Devon? I want to be angry with him."

"I know. We'll figure it out. But for now let's get you out of this room, okay?" He carefully leaned down to set my feet on the floor.

"Where are we going to go?" Tane heard the quaver in my voice and threaded his fingers through mine.

"First, we're going to go out to the bar and see if he's still here. I want you to point him out to me if he is, okay?"

"What are you going to do?"

Tane didn't answer, and instead pulled open the door and gestured me ahead. I wove my way back through the bowels of the restaurant and out to the door leading to the floor. I opened it, darting my eyes over to the bar and then ducking my head back in.

"He's not there anymore."

Tane pushed the door open and squeezed my hand. "Let's check the whole place out. Come on, I'm here with you."

One of the servers was coming in with a tray of dirty dishes, but when they saw Tane blocking the entrance, their eyes widened and they backed up.

With Tane's hand in mine, I felt more courageous and I picked my way around the restaurant, inspecting faces but turning up empty.

An odd sense of deflation hit me. He was gone.

Erin, in her black suit and heels, was walking at a quick clip toward us. "Mr. Taumata," she said, customer-service face on. "Is everything okay?" I didn't know what Tane had told her, but her eyes darted to our joined hands.

Tane ignored her, leaning toward me and meeting my eye. "When's your next shift here?"

His eyes grew sympathetic, no doubt a reaction to the dread that flooded my face. "Never is okay, if you want. We will figure something out."

I shook my head, resolute. "I work tomorrow. I have to get back to it. I'm really sorry about today, Erin."

Erin's face tightened before she schooled it down. Bitterness flooded my mouth when I remembered similar looks on the faces of my previous bosses. No one wanted to have a problem employee, even if the problem was someone else.

Without saying goodbye, Tane tugged me toward the entrance and we hit the street. It was early enough to be crowded on Queen Street, neighboring bars and clubs playing music, people walking around. I scanned the faces quickly, still not seeing Devon.

My head warred with itself. If he were here, maybe Tane would make a difference. But with Devon having disappeared again, when would he pop up next?

We were still standing on the street when I realized Tane didn't know where we were going. Did *I* know where we were going?

"Where are we going?" I said out loud.

"Your hostel."

"Okay. This way."

It was fifteen minutes to my hostel room. Tane felt like a bodyguard, my shadow, protecting me from the big bad city.

Ugh, I hoped Auckland wasn't forever ruined for me.

We arrived without incident, locking my door behind us. I slumped against the wall while Tane took a careful seat on the twin bed in my room.

He tipped his chin at my bag. "Show me a picture of him."

I pulled out my phone and turned it on, clearing the messages that popped up and navigating to Instagram. I handed the phone over. Tane squinted at the screen and scrolled for a few swipes until it buzzed in his hands. "Your sister's calling."

Before I could protest, he'd answered the call. "Hi, Iris, she's safe with me."

I swiped at the phone angrily, tossing it across the room. It smacked into the wall and bounced onto the crappy carpet.

"What the fuck, Claire!"

"How do you think Devon found me, huh?"

He drew back as if I'd slapped him. Which I nearly had. "Do you really think your sister told him?"

I could hear Iris shouting from the floor. "How else would he know? She said he'd been to see her." I wanted it to be this simple. I wanted it to be the obvious choice over him doing something more nefarious, like hacking me. And at the same time, it would crush me if it had been an innocent photo snapped of me and Tane.

I knew I wasn't thinking clearly, but if those were my three choices . . . then Iris was the one I could do something about.

Tane stood up and walked to the corner of the room, picking up my phone. "Iris," he said.

He sat down on the bed again, leaning back against the wall and closing his eyes while he listened. He grunted occasionally.

My body was winding down, the stress of the day leaving me a husk. I sat next to Tane. He pulled me sideways until we lay on the bed together, his knees bent and my head resting on his chest.

I didn't cry anymore.

But I let Tane stroke my hair and I listened to the sound of his breathing, the tinny sound of my sister's voice coming through the phone, less hysterical now.

And I fell asleep.

TWENTY-NINE

I woke up to a faint buzzing noise. My head rose and fell with Tane's chest, the buzzing coming from his pants pocket on the far side of his body.

Raising my head, I looked up at him. His mouth was set firmly in sleep, his forehead a little furrowed, as if he were trying not to wake up.

Under his hand was my phone, and when I pried it from his grasp, I found that it was dead. "Tane, wake up."

He grumbled slightly and pulled my shoulders close. "I'm awake." His eyes were still closed.

I reached down and slipped his phone out of his pocket. Nina's name lit up the screen, though his battery was nearly dead too.

"Nina?" I croaked out.

"Claire, I'm so glad to hear your voice. Are you okay?"

I propped myself up on my palm, blinking rapidly to get my senses back online. "I've been better."

"I would imagine. I spoke to your sister a few times yesterday."

"Yeah, Tane spoke to her too."

"You should call her."

I sighed. Now that it was morning, and Tane was here with me, and Devon hadn't found me here in the hostel, and I'd slept hard, I was worried.

Last night I had been angry. And scared stupid. But I needed to face the truth.

I said goodbye to Nina, plugged in my phone, and dragged myself into the tiny en suite bathroom. My hair, getting long and unkept, was sticking up in multiple directions. My eyes were crusty, my eyelids smudged from crying and mascara. I cleaned up and stepped out. Tane had stretched his legs out, his feet dangling off the end of the bed.

The room had a small desk, where my power cord was. I curled up in the desk chair, a wooden torture device, and unlocked my phone. "Tane," I said. "I'm calling Iris."

His eyes opened and he jackknifed up. "I'm awake," he said again. He shook his head like a dog and blinked off sleep.

"How did you get here anyway?"

"I flew," he said simply.

"You got here so fast."

"The flight's only an hour long, and they operate all the time. Commuter flights, even. Stop stalling and call her."

I huffed a breath but hit dial anyway. Iris picked up immediately. "Tane?"

I cleared my throat. "No, it's me."

"Claire," Iris said, and promptly burst into tears. That made me cry too . . . again. I thought I'd be all dried up by now, but sleep had replenished my tear ducts.

Between gasps, Iris told me she'd left Chris. It was him who'd told Devon where I was. For whatever reason—who was I to try to understand the inner mind of a stalker?—Devon had started to harass Iris and Chris. This was what they had been fighting about lately. Chris was tired of Devon coming around, and was sure that if they just told Devon I was halfway across the world, he'd give up.

Obviously, he hadn't.

Iris apologized over and over. And I did too. Tane rubbed my back while I listened to Iris tell me about how Devon had been coming by all the time, and she and Chris had fought more and more. Yesterday she'd confronted Chris and he had evaded answering for a while before finally admitting that when Devon had stopped coming by, it was because Chris had told him where I was.

"I am so, so sorry, Claire. I can't believe Chris would do that. He didn't think Devon would fly to find you. I didn't either, but he still doesn't have the right to know where you are."

"Where are you now, Iris? Are *you* safe?"

"I'm with a friend from work. She's letting me stay here for a couple weeks till I find my own place. Or move back to Boston. Or . . . something."

"Good, I'm glad you have a place to stay."

"What are you going to do?"

I glanced up at Tane. "I guess we're going to figure that out."

Iris and I said goodbye—she apologized for the millionth time—and Tane and I took turns using the restroom and brushing our teeth.

When he came out of the bathroom, I stood up and held out my arms. Tane slid into my embrace, running his hands over my shoulders and down my back, pulling me close and craning down to drop his chin on my head. I wrapped my arms around him, grabbing one wrist to keep my arms around his waist.

I sighed deeply. It was a good hug.

We pulled back a little bit and I looked up, resting my chin on his sternum. Tane brushed his lips against mine.

"I missed you," I told him.

"I missed you too."

"Thank you for flying up to help me. Did you at least sit in first class?"

"Ha. No."

I grimaced. "And you have to fly back, too."

"Yeah, but not for a while. I'd prefer to stay until we figure out what to do about Devon."

Pressed against my chest, Tane's stomach let out a growl. I grinned. "Maybe we should find some breakfast first. We can't plan on an empty stomach."

"And maybe we can ask about moving to a double?" Tane pulled away and offered me his hand.

"You don't want to share this little bed again?"

He eyed the single as we stepped out the door, and then he tugged me close to him in the hallway to whisper in my ear, "We'd break it."

We both laughed and made our way downstairs to find breakfast—and a bigger bed.

———

For the next few days I stuck to my work schedule. I would like to say I redeemed myself at work, but trust lost was faster than trust earned, and I could feel the other staff watching me.

Tane sat at the bar. He had a circuit of friends come and visit him; former rugby friends, buddies from school, even Emily, who kissed my cheek hard and tutted about my "troubles."

The worst part was Iris. She was constantly worried about me. I think she called Tane more often than she called me. But I didn't blame her. With Devon around, I was nervous too.

We had moved into a double room as well. Thankfully, the beds were sturdy—we tested them. Extensively.

The third morning in the new room, Tane and I were both sprawled out naked on the bed, sweat cooling on our skin. We had finally ventured out to other positions—"But I like that one," Tane had complained—and I was glad to have him with me all the time. He hadn't even mentioned Haft & Hops.

Beneath my head, Tane's stomach grumbled. I poked one of the tips of his tattoo. "Come on, let's find some food."

We spilled out into the hallway as I teased Tane about his bottomless pit of a stomach. He regularly ate three or four times what I did when we went out. He insisted on paying for all of the food while I paid for the hostel. I think I got the better deal.

Our smiles quickly faded when we heard shouting coming up the stairwell. Tane gripped my hand as we rushed down the stairs, his hand guiding me behind him when we hit the first floor. I followed Tane, but craned my neck to try to see around his bulk.

There was a scuffle, a tangle of limbs and curse words. My jaw dropped when I saw who it was: Devon. His arm was pinned behind his back by one of the German tourists I'd met when I'd first moved in—Meino, I think his name was—while one of the hotel employees batted Devon's other arm away.

"She's my girlfriend! Get off me!" Devon shouted. And then he caught sight of me, and his face turned an even darker shade of red, his eyes wild. They darted between me and Tane, who pushed me farther behind him until I couldn't see Devon anymore. "You slut!"

There was the sound of flesh connecting with flesh, a grunt of pain, and then Tane shoved me away from him. With a bizarre roar, Devon launched himself at Tane . . . who caught Devon by the face. His big palm and long arm held Devon far enough away that his punching swings were ineffective and erratic.

The comparison was stark: Tane had his game face on, cool and in control, bigger, stronger, faster; Devon was dumpy, uncoordinated, and emotional.

After a dozen or so swings, Devon lost some momentum and stalled. Tane pushed him away and took a step back, giving Devon the chance to walk away.

I saw a moment's calculation on Devon's face, the switch in tactics.

"Babe, you just need to come home," he said, bending his tone to make it sound like he was pleading. "We can work all this out. We were so good together. Do you really want to throw that all away?"

I stared at Devon for a beat, and then stepped up to take Tane's hand, twining our fingers together. Tane squeezed my hand.

"There's nothing to throw away. We were never good. And you will never win this fight."

Devon's face twisted, and I braced for a barrage of nasty words. Instead he swung a punch at Tane, who, lightning quick, headbutted Devon into a crumpled heap on the floor.

———

In the few minutes before the police arrived, we managed to find ice for Meino's black eye and tie up an unconscious Devon, and Tane sent someone out to pick up breakfast for everyone.

We gave our statements to the police, and I showed them the paperwork—well, electronic copies of the paperwork—for the restraining order in Massachusetts.

Also, I hadn't noticed the two girls in the corner of the room who had filmed the entire thing. They gave their own report and sent me and the police copies of the video.

The cops assured me that here in New Zealand, Devon wouldn't bother me again. I called Iris, who was at work, and filled her in.

She squealed in delight when I told her about the headbutting. "My hero," she said of Tane.

When I returned to Tane, he was sitting with Meino and finishing what I was pretty sure was his third breakfast burrito and laughing about something. I only caught the words *Munich* and *das boot* before I sat down on Tane's lap.

"This," I said, "is from Iris." I pressed my lips to his cheek and squeezed extra hard, squishing his face in the process. "Muah! She also says to teach me how to headbutt."

Tane looped his arm around me and gave me a squeeze. "How about a self-defense class? My rugby moves aren't going to come in handy most of the time."

"Headbutting is legal in rugby?" I asked.

"Well, no." Tane grinned. "But you learn anyway."

I slumped against Tane, tired from all the excitement. He pressed his lips against my forehead and tugged me close.

"Are you comfortable going back to work?" he murmured. "If not, my offer still stands. You'll always have a place to stay in Wellington."

I took a minute to really think about it. Seeing Devon on the ground out cold had really given me a new perspective on him, and while the managers at McGraves' hadn't been great about it at first, they'd seemed much more sympathetic to my plight after Tane had hung around the bar for a few days.

On the other hand . . . I was in love with Tane. Instead of clarifying anything, it just made everything more complicated. Being with him all the time would be amazing, but it would also burden him with taking care of me while I looked for a job, relying on him for a home. You weren't supposed to do these kinds of things to the people you loved.

I already felt terrible over Iris and her breakup with Chris. How had my mess with Devon seeped into every aspect of my life?

"I'm going to stay here," I decided. "I think that would be good for me. And the job was going well."

Tane smiled at me, and if he was disappointed, he didn't show it. "All right, let's get you ready for work, and I'll need to get back to Welly now that you're squared away."

We said goodbye to Meino, and Tane gave him his cell number to look him up if he went to Wellington. Tane packed, we said our goodbyes, and I walked into work feeling a hell of a lot better.

THIRTY

"Guess where I am," Iris said to me a few days later. I was walking to McGraves' for an opening shift, so it was mid-afternoon for Iris and I *really* didn't think she'd be this chipper at work.

I racked my brain. "Your new apartment?" I crossed my fingers, hoping she'd found a place to live. It had been a week since she and Chris had broken up, and she was very concerned about overstaying her welcome at her coworker's house.

"Nope!"

"Okay, babe, I need a hint. Are you in Chicago?"

"Technically, yes."

"Technically? What the hell does that mean?" Just then, through the phone, I heard an announcement over a loudspeaker. It sounded like a woman's voice and I swear she said, "Flight one-something-something-five to Tokyo."

"Are you at an airport?" I asked, incredulous.

"Yes!" she squealed.

Hm. Iris might be a little bit more manic than usual right now. "Okay, where are you going?"

"Bali! Which is in . . . Indo . . . Indonesia? Yes, Indonesia! Did you know Bali isn't a country? I didn't."

"You are flying to Bali?"

"Well, actually, I'm flying to Tokyo first, then Bali."

"Wait, wait, wait," I said, pinching the bridge of my nose. "Iris, what is happening right now?"

"Well, you paid me back another thousand, and I have no place to live, no boyfriend, and some vacation time saved up, so I thought, why stay here? You flew halfway around the world with no major plans because there was nothing holding you to Boston anymore. It's inspirational. Claire, *you* inspired *me.*"

"You don't have to sound so in awe about your big sister inspiring you," I grumbled.

"Oh, babe, you know what I mean."

"That still explains nothing. What the hell are you going to do in Bali?"

"Rico's in Bali."

That was the last thing I'd expected her to say and my brain literally stuttered. "Rico's in Bali? *Rico*, as in, the foreign exchange student you had a massive crush on when you were twelve? That Rico?"

"Yes," she said.

"I don't even know where to start."

"You don't have to start anywhere," Iris said, her tone turning serious. "You inspiring me is a good thing, Claire. I'm going to be out of my comfort zone, but I think it'll be exactly what I need. Like New Zealand has been good for you."

I swallowed the big lump in my throat. "I hope it is." We had a nice pause, the kind that feels like a moment where you'd hug in real life.

"So what are your plans in Bali, then?"

"Oh, I have no idea."

The statement was so unlike her that I burst out laughing. She told me Rico was the one with the plans. He'd been traveling solo for nearly a year, and my sister, my brave, ballsy sister, had called him up and invited herself along on his trip.

I'd known that they were still close friends who kept in touch through the years like new age pen pals, but she hadn't mentioned Rico in a while. Talk had tapered off once she'd started dating Chris, and I wondered if that was her decision or Chris's influence, but it didn't matter now.

"All I know is that we are going on a boat somewhere. Actually, it's two nights in Bali, and then we fly . . . somewhere else in Indonesia to get on a boat? Anyway, like I said, Rico has made a plan."

"And you can afford this with the money I paid you back?"

"Well . . . Rico offered to help me out a little bit. You know, you might be able to learn a thing or two from me, Claire."

"I thought I was the one who inspired you? Why you gotta turn the tables on me?"

She laughed. "You know, when you came to me asking for help, I had no problem lending you the money. And Rico's done the same for me. I asked him for help, and he's helping me. It's what you do for people you love."

"So how can I help you?"

"Not me, you doofus. You."

"Me?"

"You *want* to be in Wellington. Tane's offered to help you, and you love him. Why shouldn't you accept his help?" Tane had begrudgingly gone back to Wellington after Devon was arrested, but we'd talked every day between shifts and obligations.

"I don't want to take advantage of him."

"But," Iris said gently, "he's offering. Don't you think he'll get something out of this too?"

It was on the tip of my tongue to make a joke—banging-hot sex, of course—but I knew what Iris meant. I loved Tane. And I'd make sure he knew it.

I heard another announcement in the background and Iris interrupted my thoughts. "Okay, babe, that's my flight. Gotta run."

"Message me when you find Rico so I know you're safe."

"Will do. But then don't expect to hear from me for a week. I'll be on vacay! Love you."

"Love you too."

I shook my head after hanging up the phone. Look at us Bailey girls, out on adventures beyond anything we'd ever imagined. Who would have thought?

———

It took me two days to convince myself that Iris was right, that I belonged in Wellington with Tane. I gave my two weeks' notice at McGraves', but it ended up being a four-day notice. Auckland was flush with people needing jobs in the off-season, so my shifts were quickly picked up by everyone else.

And I splurged. I booked a flight from Auckland to Wellington. Monday morning I said my goodbyes to the friends I'd collected in Auckland—basically the hostel staff and Meino —and took an Uber to the airport.

If my sister could take a break from everything causing stress in her life, I could too. And while I was definitely going to pay her back, it helped knowing that she was with someone who would help her out just as I would.

My flight was quick and I took the bus to Haft & Hops. Tane called once, but I ignored it. I'd see him soon, and this was better in person.

By the time I was walking through the front door, it was mid-afternoon. A few customers were in the main room and one of the servers, Ash, was behind the bar, fiddling with her phone.

"Hey, Ash," I called as I walked past, dragging my luggage behind me.

"Hey, cuz," she said as I typed in the code for Tane's door. I collapsed the suitcase's handle and hoisted it up to climb the stairs. When I hit the top, I knocked and opened the door. "Tane! You home?"

I stepped into the room and froze. The bed wasn't just unmade—it was stripped of bedding. The closet door was open, a few boxes were stacked to the side, but otherwise the room was empty. Personal effects were gone, counters bare, rugby memorabilia missing.

"No way," Nina said from the open doorway, her mouth gaping open.

"Nina? Where's Tane?" My brow furrowed in concern. I didn't understand what was happening here.

Nina didn't help when she burst out laughing. "Oh. My. God. I thought this only happened in the movies. What are you doing here?"

"Tane offered me a place to stay if I ever needed one. And . . . well, I don't need it. But I want to be here instead."

Nina didn't say anything, and instead brought up her phone and pressed some buttons without breaking eye contact with me. I heard the phone ring, and Tane cut in. Nina held the phone in front of her: a video call.

"Nina? I'm just getting back to Mom's. I couldn't find her. I went by McGraves' and they said Claire quit. She's not at the hostel, either, so it's like she's disappeared, and then she didn't answer my call. What if something happened to her?" Tane's voice was edged in panic and my stomach plummeted. He was in Auckland.

"Bro," Nina said, turning around so I was in the shot. "Claire's here."

Tane's shocked face took up the entire screen as he leaned in and squinted. "Claire, what are you doing there?"

I gestured down to the rolling suitcase at my feet. "I packed up all my stuff and came to find you."

Shock and awe passed over Tane's face for a moment, but then he turned away and I heard the click of a car door opening. The phone bounced around until Tane held it up at arm's length, showing me his shoulders, chest, and the bed of his truck full of boxes and strapped-down items. And a broad, happy smile. "I packed up all my stuff and came to find you. I was going to stay with my mum until we sorted something else out."

"Oh my God," I said, and laughed, pressing my hands to my flushing cheeks.

Nina shook her head, exasperated. "You two are so cute, it's annoying. Tane, call Claire.

Claire, answer your phone. I'm going back to the bar."

Nina closed the door behind her and while her footsteps were still echoing down the stairwell, my phone rang.

"I hear my boyfriend's an idiot," I said into the phone as I answered, my voice colored with affection.

"How's that?"

"He gave up this sweet apartment above the bar he owns to move across a very small country for some American girl."

He chuckled in my ear. "I suppose the move-across-the-country grand gesture is more impactful in the States."

"Your plan was to live with your mom and then what? What would you do all day while I went to work?"

"Do you want to hear my plan, or do you want me to drive back to Wellington?"

"Aw, Tane," I said. "You just drove eight hours. Stay the night with your mom—or however long you want to—and then come back. I'll restart the job hunt and we'll figure the rest out."

"I like driving," he insisted.

"I know you do. But sixteen hours in a day is too much."

He grumbled for a moment but then agreed. "Here's my plan, then. Have you heard of a dry bar?"

THIRTY-ONE

Tane stayed only one night in Auckland before making the drive back. When I woke up after sleeping on sheets borrowed from Nina, I unpacked and then went downstairs to the bar and found her making breakfast for the two of us.

"Toast," Nina directed me, pointing to my usual spot by the toaster. "My mum is *thrilled*. She actually called me last night to gossip about you two. She said Tane was all moony and happy last night."

I smiled down at the toaster, blushing.

"Oh. Em. Gee. You are all moony too. Ack!" She waved a hand. "So cute! Have you heard from Tane this morning?"

"Yes, he left Auckland a couple of hours ago."

"And what about your sister? Was she super excited? I messaged her, but I haven't heard back."

"Right, about that. Iris is in Indonesia. Without internet."

"What?" Nina squawked, and I filled her in on my globe-trotting sister.

"She said she was flying to a different island, but she didn't know which one. I literally have no idea where she is right now. Or in which time zone. Hmm." I pulled up a time zone map, but Indonesia was a much bigger country than I'd expected. It had three time zones.

I texted her. *Sooo . . . I'm back in Wellington. Quit my job. Moved in with Tane. Well . . . sorta.*

Tane has to move back in. It's a lot to explain. Call me. I hope Indonesia and Rico are fantastic! Tell him I said hi.

After breakfast, I used the office computer while Nina got the bar ready to open. Some of the staff did double takes when walking by and then stopped to chat, so I kept getting distracted. But I did submit more job applications, made some phone calls, and did some research for Tane's big plan.

Tane wanted to open a sister bar to Haft & Hops, possibly in Wellington but most likely in Auckland. Instead of serving alcohol, the bar would be a sober—or dry—bar. I hadn't known any dry bars in Boston, but I also hadn't known to look for them. An entire bar subculture revolved around nonalcoholic drinks like the craft cocktails I'd made or the beer we'd tried at Haft & Hops.

And there wasn't a dry bar in New Zealand.

I was daydreaming about new cocktail recipes when my phone rang next to me. Iris's photo looked up at me and I quickly answered the video call.

"Oh. My. God. Claire! I am so furious with you!" She squinted at me, trying to look threatening, I suppose, but the corners of her lips weren't cooperating and she just looked constipated instead.

"What? What did I do?"

"I finally connected to the internet today and I had about fifty messages from Nina documenting the saga of Tane and Claire. 'He's going to Auckland,' 'She showed up here.' I get *one* text from you like, 'Oh hey, I guess I live with my boyfriend now.' I. Need. Details."

I laughed and filled Iris in on everything that had happened since her vacation from reality had started.

"So the place is entirely empty except for my clothes in two drawers of the dresser and my toiletries in the bathroom. It's actually more like he's moving in with me. I've staked my side of the bed and the shelves in the vanity."

"And Tane gets in tonight? And you're going to open a bar together?"

"Well, no," I corrected her. "By the time Tane gets a loan and finds a property, I'll probably be back in America."

"Sure, that's what you think," Iris said coyly.

"My visa is up in five months. Less than five months, actually," I pointed out. "I will have to leave the country."

"Sure, sure, and there's no way to make your stay indefinite."

My stomach fluttered at Iris's insinuation. "I don't know what you're talking about. How is Indonesia?"

"Claire! You're so chickenshit, you won't even say the word. Get married!"

"I'm not having a green card—or whatever the New Zealand equivalent is—wedding."

"Babe, it's not a green card marriage. You and Tane love each other. That's literally what those visas are for. So you can stay in the country with the person you love."

"Shut it, Iris. It's months away. We might break up by then. Besides, I would miss you too much. Being on the other side of the world from you was always supposed to be a temporary state."

"Okay, true. But as much as I like having you nearby, I would suffer for true love."

I rolled my eyes.

"You know I can see you, right?"

I smirked at her. "So, how's Rico?"

Well . . ." Iris said. "About that . . ."

"Iris," I warned her. "Spill."

"We slept together."

The seconds ticked by. I was stunned and speechless.

"Ex*cuse* me? You gave me all that shit about not updating you even though you were unavailable and now I find out I didn't even get so much as a text message?! It's only been a few days. How did this happen?"

"Come on, Claire, don't be like that. And it's not just a few days. It's Rico. We've known each other for a decade. I thought he was so cute when I was thirteen, but oh my God, he's so hot now. And our very first night in Bali they just assumed we were a couple and gave us the honeymoon suite and it was so romantic."

"You slept with him on the first night?"

"Judgy McJudgerFace. It was the second," she huffed.

I loved how Iris had given me absolutely no information about her trip other than she slept with Rico. Which I suppose was fair, because I could hardly stop thinking about Tane.

"I'm really happy for you," I told her. "I'm just surprised. Wow."

"I know. But"—her tone became more solemn—"I think that was it for us. I don't know. He's kind of . . ."

Iris thought for a little bit before continuing. "He's kind of a loner. He's got these plans to be in an apartment somewhere in Bali and just surf every day, which is like, great, but . . . I don't see how I would fit into that."

"Have you talked about the future? How long will he be in Bali?"

"Another month or so. But, like, I have a job and stuff back in Chicago."

I leaned forward in the office chair. "Come on, you just told me that whatever I want to do, I should do it, and figure out how to make it work. What do you want?"

Her voice was much firmer when she said, "I want to be a teacher."

"Good. Then go be a teacher, Iris. Figure out how to make that work."

She took a deep breath. "Yeah, yeah. You are right."

"I know I am." I smirked at her. "Okay, so, for real this time, how is Indonesia?"

By the time I'd hung up with Iris, I'd gotten a pretty picture in my head of her time exploring. She talked a lot about monkeys and jungles and manta rays, and, honestly, it sounded like her and Rico had crammed more into their one-week vacation in Indonesia than I had during my entire time in New Zealand.

But their adventure wasn't over, and neither was mine.

A knock came from the door and I pushed away from the desk. "Come in, Nina, I'm done—"

But it wasn't Nina who came through the door: it was Tane.

"What?" I squealed—which might have been the first time I had ever squealed in my life—and leaped into his arms. "You got here so fast."

"Mum loaded me up with coffee and sent me out early," he said, pressing a kiss to my lips. "I checked upstairs for you first and saw that you've taken over my side of the bed."

"It's my side now." I slid down his body. "You abandoned it."

Tane cocked his head and studied my face. "How are you feeling about all this? Living with me, not paying rent, not having a job just yet?"

"If I think about it too much, it's scary. But here's the thing." I looked down at my hands, fisted in his shirt, and I suddenly felt shy. I sucked in a deep breath and, in a fake-it-till-you-make-it move, tilted my chin up with confidence. "I love you."

Tane's smile was slow and warm. "I love you too." He planted a firm kiss on my lips. "And I'm glad you are seeing reason now. I've wanted you here so bad."

"Yeah?" My cheeks hurt, I was smiling so hard.

"Yeah."

"Well then, kiss me." I tilted my head up, demanding more kisses.

He did kiss me . . . for a little while. And then we had to move all his things back in, so between trips up the stairs and over boxes of books and dishes and memorabilia, I told Tane about my sister and Rico, and their plans.

"She thinks we should get married," I said, watching Tane's face for a reaction. He gave me none. "Not now," I continued, "but when my visa is up. That would be weird, right?"

"Weird? Marrying someone you love?"

I put my fist on my hip. "Did you talk to Iris somehow? That's exactly what she said."

Tane smirked at me while putting a stack of plates back in his cabinet. "No, but it's logical."

The box in front of me was full of carefully wrapped picture frames, so I pulled one out, unwrapping it. A team photo stared up at me. "Where should these go?"

"You've made yourself at home. Put them where you think they should go and we can always move things around later."

I stood up and carried the frame over to the bookshelf and placed it on an empty spot. "What do you think about marriage? As a general idea?"

When I turned around, Tane shrugged. "I'd never thought about getting married before. I was too busy with rugby and random dates to get invested in someone. But my parents had a good marriage. Nina and Hemi, despite being absolutely nothing alike, make marriage look easy. They are still both themselves, but they support each other."

Hm. Well, Tane and I were cut from the same cloth. Our marriage would be different from theirs. If we got married. But it was becoming a lot easier to see the two of us forty years from now, being old and grumpy together.

"I have to admit," Tane continued, "I have a hard time seeing you as a bride. I don't think I've ever seen you wear anything white. Or lace. Or sequined." He squinted, like he was trying to imagine it.

I laughed and threw balled-up Bubble Wrap at him, but it didn't get very far. "I can dress up. But I always pictured a courthouse wedding. I don't want a big party."

"So how about it?" Tane said. "One month before your visa runs out. If we're still together, we'll get married."

"At the courthouse?"

"At the courthouse."

"No big party, no lacy dress, no guests?"

"None of those things."

I crossed the room, leaning against the small counter between Tane's living room and kitchen, resting on my elbows. He mirrored me on the other side.

"I like the way you propose, Tane Taumata." I pressed a kiss to his lips.

"I like the way you accept, Claire Bailey, or maybe Claire Taumata."

I smiled up at him. "You, sir, are looking very confident."

His eyes twinkled. "I am pretty confident that I can convince you to stay in New Zealand. You've still got a lot to explore, and I'm going to make sure you love it."

And I was pretty confident too. Between Tane and New Zealand itself, somehow I was finding my place.

EPILOGUE

"Your sister is going to kill me. My sister is going to kill me," Tane said, tugging at the sleeves of his suit.

"Don't worry," I said cheerfully. "They'll probably coordinate it."

We walked toward the front of the courthouse in Wellington, ready to see a judge and get officially married. It all seemed a little surreal even though we had talked about it months ago. For the last few months, my ability to call

Tane my boyfriend had an expiration date—either I left the country or we got married.

So we were getting married.

Granted that wasn't going to solve everything. Turns out, partnership visas are pretty hard to get in New Zealand. But this was a start, and Tane and I were committed to staying together.

I had always thought that Iris would get married first, to Chris. But now that my sister had gone full-on vagabond, I had no idea what her thoughts were on marriage.

Man, I really missed her. I needed to see her soon, remind myself in person that even if she'd made huge changes in her life, she was still the same sister, my best friend and my staunch supporter.

Tane and I reached the stairs leading up to the courthouse and I threaded my fingers through his. Dry & Draught had opened two weeks ago here in Wellington, but I had only a month left on my visa. We had stuck to our proposal—no party, no guests.

We hadn't told anyone that we were getting married today. Just a government official and a witness.

I had stressed over the decision, but Tane assured me that his family would understand— Emily had already done the mother-of-the-bride thing, and Tane felt like he was free and clear.

He also assured me that we would, indeed, have a honeymoon. It would just be a bit delayed. We were too busy with the bar to take time off now, but six months from today we would fly out for a week of honeymooning in Fiji.

We had not stuck to our agreement about attire, though, and I had surprised Tane with my dress. No, it wasn't sequined, but it was mid-thigh, off-white, and lacy. The crew neck fit me perfectly and it wasn't often that I'd fallen in love with clothes. But somehow the idea of a dress sat in the back of my mind and when I saw it shopping one day, I had to have it.

Tane's suit was crisp and gray pin-striped, reminding me of the pictures of him online at special events during his career. He confessed that it wasn't one of those suits—they didn't fit him anymore—and he'd gotten a new one.

While the temperature in spring was fairly mild, the damn winds were still constant and they had extra bite. I had a black wrap draped over my shoulders to try to fight the chill from the car to the building.

Tane opened the door for me and I stepped inside, immediately feeling relief from the wind. We talked to the person working the security desk and followed the signs to find the right office. We turned a corner and Tane and I both froze in place.

Our sisters were waiting outside the door.

Iris was waiting outside the door.

"Surprise!" she whisper-shouted in the marble hallway.

I glanced up at Tane, who was just as shocked as I was, and back to our sisters. "How did you know?"

"Oh please," Nina said. "You both marked today off, and Claire went all gooey-eyed when she saw that dress."

Okay, I *had* been shopping with Nina when I saw the dress in a thrift store, but I thought I'd hid my interest well enough. I'd left it on the rack, but circled back to the store hours later and bought it.

And insisting that we get married one month before the expiration of my visa meant that Tane and I had both taken off on a Saturday— unheard of. So maybe we weren't very discreet.

We finally unfroze as our sisters walked toward us with arms outstretched for hugs.

"Is it too much?" Iris whispered. "If you really don't want us here, that's okay."

"No, no, I'm happy. We didn't say anything because we didn't want to make a big deal about it. I thought that there was no way you'd be able to come. Especially since it's going to be a half-hour ceremony and no party. It's a long way for you to fly."

We pulled back and swapped huggers. Nina squeezed me extra hard. "Look," she said, "I know you can't play favorites with sisters. If you invite one of us, you have to invite the other, and yada yada. I already have the leg up since we work together."

I didn't technically work with or for Nina and Tane, but unofficially, I was very involved in Dry & Draught. I created the menus and often went with Nina while meeting with vendors. All this around my *other* job, working at a restaurant on the harbor. Patience had been the key, and after five weeks of jobless living with Tane, I'd gotten a call offering me a position as an events bartender—if I could get to the location in an hour.

It wasn't a complex job, mostly beer and wine, but I got to balance it with menu creation for Dry & Draught.

When Nina stepped away, I realized they weren't the only ones in the hallway. Hemi and a tall Latino man—Rico, I assumed—stood off to the side, Hemi talking animatedly about something. Yes, Hemi was *animated*.

Iris leaned in. "Nina's husband is such a talker."

I looked at Nina. "Did you hear that? Your husband's a talker?"

"He talks to me all the time, Claire. I think he's a little intimidated by you."

I got hugs from both men, and then we were called into the office for the official ceremony. It was in English and Māori, and since I didn't have any flowers, I had my hands entwined with Tane's as we listened and said our I do's.

The officiant, a heavyset woman with a moko kauae on her chin, said something in Māori that she didn't translate. But she didn't need to. Tane followed instructions and swept me up into a firm and chaste kiss.

———

"So you flew all the way here from Phuket. Was it worth it?" I teased Iris.

She shoved my shoulder, causing me to teeter on the barstool at Dry & Draught. After the very short ceremony, we'd reconvened at the bar to celebrate.

"We're staying a week—well, only five more days, because we've been here for two. And I don't just want to see the ceremony. I want to see the life you've built here." She gestured around at Dry & Draught. "Look at everything you helped create."

"Wait, you've been here two days already? What have you been doing?" I took a sip of a nonalcoholic white wine. I hardly ever drank wine, but it seemed like a good thing to do while wearing a fancy lace dress on my wedding day.

"We're staying with Nina, of course."

I rolled my eyes. Those two were thick as.

Okay, maybe I still had paperwork to fill out before I was officially a Kiwi, but I was starting to think like one.

"And I had to buy appropriate clothes," she continued. "Rico and I are pretty much beach bums. All I do is attend school online while Rico surfs or kiteboards, and then we usually go to the beach or walk around the Old Town. I didn't have anything wedding-appropriate."

I looked her over. Iris wore a pale floral wrap dress, sensible flats, and a chunky turquoise necklace. Her hair, black like mine, was pulled back in a low bun, whereas mine was just getting long enough to brush the tops of my shoulders. It was too short to ponytail, too long to stay back.

Iris was getting a certificate so she could teach English in Asia; she and Rico were hoping to move to Japan. The classes and the lifestyle were working pretty well; she also had a glow about her. And I told her so.

"Well," she said, leaning in and dropping her voice, "you have a certain glow too. Look at us, the two Bailey sisters. Who would have thought?"

I smiled, and looked down the bar. Rico was next to Iris, and across from him, behind the bar, was Tane. We were tucked away in our own little corner while Nina flitted around, running things so we wouldn't have to. Hemi had gone back to their house to pick up the girls and Emily and bring them back to the bar, where we were going to order takeout for an early dinner before things got crowded.

Tane had rolled his sleeves up, showing off those thick forearms I loved so much. He laughed at something Rico said, and tipped back his glass of beer for a sip. We'd discovered some much better nonalcoholic beers now that we had stronger connections to nonalcoholic producers. Stocking an entire bar's worth of drinks opened doors.

Tane caught my eye and winked at me. My husband. He moved toward me and leaned over for a kiss. My charming sister whooped loud enough to startle some nearby guests and I shushed her.

"I have a wedding present for you," Tane said. "Or, the idea of a wedding present."

I gave him a little side-eye. "I thought we said no presents."

"You can say no if you want. But I reached out to the guy who did my most recent tattoos, and he's still operating here in Wellington. He's pretty confident he can take a look at your tattoo and design a *kirituhi*—that's a Māori-style tattoo for someone without Māori blood—to cover your old one up. If you want."

I swooned. "Aw, that would be amazing. Thank you, babe."

Forks and glasses clinked around us, started by Nina, who stood behind Tane. We kissed again.

Emily burst through the front door, Hemi and girls in tow, and began enthusiastic hugs and kisses for us all. My new family moved over to a lounge area where the adults could chat and the girls could play on the low tables.

Iris was right: Look at everything I'd built. I'd come to New Zealand frustrated, broke, and running.

Now I had more family than I'd ever imagined, a husband I loved, and soon, when I was officially here on a spousal visa, I would quit the events job and work here full-time. At the bar Tane and I had built together.

And I was going to go home with a hot rugby player every night for the rest of my life.

The End

I haven't seen my best friend in ten years. That massive crush? Still alive and well.

Want to read about Iris and Rico? Their short story, The Best Friend in Indonesia, is free for newsletter subscribers. Download your copy by scanning here:

Newsletter subscribers also get bonus epilogues and a behind-the-scenes look at the trips that inspired my stories.

AUTHOR'S NOTE

Dear Reader,

Domestic violence doesn't recognize borders. If you or someone you know needs help while overseas, please consider reaching out to your nearest embassy or consulting the Hot Peach Pages, an international list of agencies that may be able to help.

Additionally, everyone's journey with alcohol is different. While a sobriety coach and a solid support network helped Tane achieve his goals, remember—he's a fictional character. If you need help with sobriety, consider Alcoholics Anonymous.

Please Review

Reviews are critical to all authors. You can leave a review for *The Player in New Zealand* at all retailers
Amazon | Apple | Kobo
Barnes & Noble | Google Books
and
Goodreads | BookBub

Also by Liz Alden:

<u>The Love and Wanderlust Series</u>
The Night in Lover's Bay (free prequel short story)
The Fling in Panama
The Slow Burn in Polynesia
The Second Chance in the Mediterranean
The Rival in South Africa (standalone novella)
The Player in New Zealand
The Best Friend in Indonesia (free standalone short story)

<u>Aged Like Fine Wine Series</u>
Rosé with My Fake Fiancé
Riesling with My Roommate
Prosecco with My Professor
Cava with My Colleague

<u>Holiday Retellings Series</u>
Nutcracker with Benefits
Frosty Proximity

<u>Wanderlust Resort Series</u>
Beach Boss (free standalone short story)
Beach Resolution
Put it in Beach Mode

<u>Standalones</u>
The Boudoir Arrangement

ACKNOWLEDGMENTS

It's very flattering to have the support of so
many fun and interesting authors. Thank you to
Ellie White, Karen Grey, Marty Vee, and Lillian
Lark, who read early versions of this book. Their
help was invaluable. Additional thanks to the
Kiwi authors who read this book for accuracy:
Jax Calder, who writes wonderful gay romance
featuring rugby players, and Stephanie Ruth.
Also thank you to my sensitivity readers, Liam
Stevens from Toa Tabletop and Ranui Calman.

I continue to adore my editing team: Tiffany,
who put many hours into this manuscript and
told me we don't pick favorites but *this one
might be it;* Kaitlin, who patiently points out my

bad habits; and Annette, who strives to make
my work spotless (and often succeeds!).

And of course, Elizabeth. Thank you for making
me giggle every time I see the cover.

And as always, a big thank-you to my husband,
who encouraged me so much from day one,
and my parents, all five of them, who supported
this book in one way or another.

ABOUT THE AUTHOR

Liz Alden is a digital nomad. Most of the time she's on her sailboat, but sometimes she's in Texas. She knows exactly how big the world is —having sailed around it—and exactly how small it is, having bumped into friends worldwide.

She's been a dishwasher, an engineer, a CEO, and occasionally gets paid to write or sail.

The books in the Love and Wanderlust series are inspired by her real-life travel.

Follow Liz:
LizAlden.com